P9-CEH-667

HIGH PRIESTESS

Also by David Skibbins

EIGHT OF SWORDS

To Doug + family

HIGH
PRIESTESS

DAVID SKIBBINS

Thanks so much
for your wonderful
support - I hope you
enjoy adventure
#2

THOMAS DUNNE BOOKS
ST. MARTIN'S MINOTAUR
NEW YORK

THOMAS DUNNE BOOKS
An imprint of St. Martin's Press.

HIGH PRIESTESS. Copyright © 2006 by David Skibbins. All rights reserved.
Printed in the United States of America. No part of this book may be used or
reproduced in any manner whatsoever without written permission except in
the case of brief quotations embodied in critical articles or reviews. For information, address St. Martin's Press, 175 Fifth Avenue, New York, N.Y. 10010.

www.minotaurbooks.com

Library of Congress Cataloging-in-Publication Data [TK]

ISBN 0-312-35233-6
EAN 978-0-312-35233-2

First Edition: April 2006

10 9 8 7 6 5 4 3 2 1

High Priestess *is dedicated to two politicians who make me proud to be an American:*

On September 14, 2001, one member of Congress took a stand in opposition to every other senator and representative to speak against giving President Bush unlimited power to launch wars in the Mideast. **Congresswoman Barbara Lee** *said, "We must be careful not to embark on an open-ended war with neither an exit strategy nor a focused target. We cannot repeat past mistakes. . . . As we act, let us not become the evil that we deplore."*

On January 7, 2005, one senator stood against all her fellow senators to insist that a debate ensue about the corrupt irregularities in the United States electoral process. **Senator Barbara Boxer** *said, "We cannot keep turning our eyes away from a flawed system, particularly as we have people dying in Iraq every day to bring democracy to those people."*

Warren Ritter and I salute the courage of both these women.

ACKNOWLEDGMENTS

So many fine readers and editors tear my work apart in the service of making it readable and enjoyable. Thank you: Laura Kennedy, P. J. Coldren, Mary Ellen Johnson, Jerry and Sally Skibbins, Harriet Sage, Heather Skibbins, my tough agent Jennifer Jackson, and the world's best mystery editor Ruth Cavin. Also thanks to the rest of the crew at St. Martin's, especially Toni Plummer and Linda McFall. I'd like to thank Julia Spencer-Fleming and her husband, Ross Hugo-Vidal, for being outstanding, generous mentors in this field. I thank Joel Crockett, co-owner of Four Eyed Frog Bookstore, and all the other supportive independent booksellers it's been my pleasure to get to know. Finally, it's all very simple: I could not write without the abiding love and ongoing support of my wife, Marla Skibbins. And Warren has two words to say to everyone on this list, "You Rock!"

CHAPTER ONE

When was he going to get here? For what seemed like the hundredth time, she looked down the path. Empty.

God, she hated this weather! Her head was covered in sweat under her wig. The hot wind tossed dust into her colored contact lenses and dried out her skin. She was going to look like a mummy before this was over.

It was a good thing this guy lived on routine, because only a complete idiot would be out here hiking in 98 degrees. But, rain or shine, Richard Steed could be counted on to drag the sorry ass of his aging Labrador retriever over the Marin hills. She'd watched him for a week. Same path, same time, like clockwork.

She heard the bark of his dog before she saw them round the bend below. He was decked out in his L.L. Bean khaki hiking shorts, matching shirt with mesh venting on the sides, and Adidas cross-trainers. He had the Flexi-lead in one hand and a mahogany walking stick in the other.

She was already sitting on the ground in the middle of the path, tying a bandana around her ankle. Soft sobs escaped from her huddled figure.

"Are you okay?" He had reined in his dog and was standing over her.

She glanced up and then turned her attention back to tightening her bandage. Pitching her voice a little more shrill than normal she said, "No, I think I might have a really bad sprained ankle. I don't think it's broken, though."

"Do you need any help?"

"If you could just help me get up, I think I'll be okay."

He told his dog, "Stay, Stella." He reached down to grip her arm. He was positioned perfectly: facing her, back to the edge of the sheer drop behind him. She let him pull her up and waited until he let go of her arm. She watched him tilt his head, furrow his brows, and begin to speak. Centering her energy she pushed out hard on his chest with both arms. He went over cleanly and only just began a scream before she heard a deep crunching thump. Then all she could hear was the incessant barking of the dog as his bitch ran up and down the path, looking for a route to her master.

She untied the bandana from her ankle and began jogging down to the parking lot at the trailhead. Next time would be even easier.

CHAPTER TWO

Do you believe in evil?"

The man sitting across the card table from me looked like a clean-shaven Santa Claus: corpulent, with rosy cheeks, sparkling blue eyes, and a wide friendly smile.

"Evil?"

"Yes; the wicked, corrupt, perverted intention to harm another person." He still wore his merry grin.

"Well, I've met people who delight in creating suffering for others, so I guess, by that definition, I do."

"And what about evil that transcends the individual personality, Evil with a capital 'E'? The universal adversary to good. Do you believe that there is an inherent malicious force in the universe?"

"Look Mr. Hightower, I don't have any idea. I'm just a tarot card reader, not a theologian."

He interrupted me. "You may call me Edward. And if I wanted to pose these questions to a religious scholar, Berkeley is awash in divinity students and professors. I know who you are, Mr. Ritter. It matters to me what you believe."

"You can call me Warren. Well, Edward, I don't know what I actually believe about universal evil. Give me a sec to think about it."

Edward nodded. "By all means, take as long as you need."

I leaned back in my folding chair. My "office" was a portable wooden table located on the sidewalk at the corner of Telegraph and Haste in the middle of downtown Berkeley, California.

There is a legendary village in Scotland that was "blessed" two hundred years ago. This blessing took the form of a spell that made Brigadoon exist only one day every century. If we were to wander into it we would be back in eighteenth-century Scotland.

Berkeley too, was "blessed," but it often feels more like a curse. In the sixties it was home to the free speech movement and the People's Park riots. It was the heart of the youth revolution. Sometimes it looks as though nothing has changed in four decades. You can still wander into head shops along Telegraph Avenue. Long-haired street vendors outside are pushing stained-glass ornaments, silver earrings, and tie-dyed T-shirts all decorated in peace symbols. Protestors still troop down the street singing songs and carrying signs.

But the sixties are ancient history. Today the earrings are made in sweatshops in China. The head shops are run by Arabs. Most shoppers are headed for the Gap and the Shoe Factory. The university has rolled back admission practices to those of the fifties, and the student body gets whiter and richer every year.

My client was immobile, eyes locked on me, waiting for me to speak. I looked away.

I became aware of the cacophony of sounds around me: the grind of an under-shifted U-Haul truck, two drifters yelling greetings at each other across the traffic, the excited chatter of a flock of freshman girls in the crosswalk. I love chaos. The up-roar was music to me and the stench of exhaust, perfume.

It was the first weekend of the fall semester. Hotter than hell. Just then gust tried to blow all my cards off the table. Damn this nasty, incessant wind. It had been roasting the Bay Area for weeks. In Italy they call it Scirocco; in Germany, the Foehn; in Australia, Brickfielder. In Southern California it's known as the Santa Ana. Up here around San Francisco we say "It's firestorm weather." Then we look nervously to the hills, hills that were scorched in '91 in a fire so hot that it melted automobile en-gines, bent steel I-beams, killed twenty-five people, and left an-other five thousand homeless. Some people call it the Diablo, blowing in from the direction of our local extinct volcano. The Native Americans had it about right. They called it "the bitter wind."

Suicides were up, divorces were up, and homicide seemed a damn fine idea. I keep about twenty crystals and geodes around the edge of my table. They are not for show. In this weather I set them on top of every card I lay on the table, hoping to anchor my cards against some merciless blast of air.

Business had been brisk. Students facing life's imponderable problems looked to me for a transpersonal perspective: "Does he love me?" "Should I major in psychology?" "Do sororities suck, or are they a good idea?"

This was a hundred-and-fifty-dollar day, for sure. I wanted to short-circuit the philosophy discussion and finish this reading with Santa before the felon wind lifted up my whole table and

5

made off with it. My client looked familiar, in a way that made me a little uneasy. I never realized how much I disliked St. Nick before.

"Edward, I don't know much about the universal nature of reality. I've never met God or Satan and I doubt the existence of anything more powerful than chance and chaos. But I'm pretty ignorant. There are more things in heaven and earth than are dreamt of in my philosophy. So I try to keep an open mind. Now getting back to your cards, what I see—"

Again he interrupted me. "That was a humble answer, Warren. And I liked the *Hamlet* reference. That is appropriate to my proposition. You see I'm not really here to get a reading. I want to hire you for another matter entirely. And it has to do with 'murder most foul.'"

This was very annoying. "Wait right there, Ed. You must be under some misunderstanding about me. I read tarot cards on weekends. That's it. If you need help with some criminal matter you need to take it up with the police or with a private eye or with anyone else besides me. And if you don't want a reading please feel free to move along, and let someone else take your seat."

He took an envelope out of his pocket and put it on the table. "This will more than make up for your loss of revenue while you hear me out, Warren."

It was time to get shitty. "Call me Mr. Ritter. Your money is of no interest to me, Mr. Hightower. I do not involve myself with police business. Now, please get up and leave."

He put a smoky quartz crystal on top of the envelope to weigh it down. He made no move to leave. His eyes never left mine. "This spring you were *very* involved with police business:

kidnapping, auto theft, murder. I understand that you want to put all that behind you. You'd like to return to a life of quiet anonymity. But I am in acute need of your many non-mystical talents. All I ask is that you hear me out. At the end of my presentation you may say no and I will get up, leave quietly, and you may pocket the five hundred dollars in that envelope."

This guy was trouble. I wanted no part of it. I didn't need his blood money. Back in the seventies I had parlayed my thirty pieces of silver into a comfortable Microsoft nest egg. I worked for my own enjoyment, not out of desperation.

Hightower was right; a few months ago I'd been embroiled in a messy police investigation. I wanted no repeat performances. I didn't need that kind of grief. "No. I'm not interested. Take your money and move on."

He looked directly at me. "I ask you to reconsider, Mr. Green."

Oh shit! He knew who I was.

My birth name is Richard Green. In my youth, I'd been a leader of a very left-wing street guerrilla group. Thirty years ago I buried the name Green, along with all my connections to my past. Or so I thought.

I stared at him for a minute.

"Okay, Eddie, you win. But no blackmail. I don't know how you got that name, but I never want to hear you use it again. I'll listen to you and that's it. If I'm not interested in your proposition you agree to walk off, right?"

"Correct."

"And you already know I probably won't help you, right?"

"Correct again." He folded his hands together on the table in a prayer-like gesture.

"Okay, thanks for the donation. Now make it quick. Shoot."

But before anybody could shoot anything, a high-pitched voice yelled out, *"You murderer! Rot in hell, you son of a bitch!"*

Nothing unusual in this outburst. Back in 1967, then-Governor Reagan had the brilliant idea to shut down the state mental hospitals and save the state a ton of money. He told everyone not to worry, the local community mental health centers could handle the flood of crazy folks. Then, as president, he cut funding for community mental health centers. More than any other human being, Ronnie was responsible for creating the mentally ill homeless problem in the United States.

Many of these people made their own way to Berkeley. Many more were sent here with one-way bus tickets from Ohio or Arkansas, paid for by out-of-state social workers. Berkeley is one of the only communities in the United States that spends a significant chunk of its ever-shrinking public monies on medical care, therapy, and job services for the homeless.

Telegraph Avenue is known as "the open ward." We witness psychotic outbursts every few hours. I casually glanced over at the screaming nut case, and saw how wrong I was this time.

An attractive Asian woman in her twenties, with short dark hair and long red fingernails, was leaning out of the cockpit of her BMW Z-3 and directing her attack at my client. Homeless people don't usually drive Z-3s.

I looked back at Edward. He studied her and then folded his hands and looked down at the table. She was just warming up, continuing to scream at him: "You'll burn for eternity if I have anything to say about it!"

The drivers behind her began hitting their horns, and a

black guy in a delivery truck started to yell at her. She hit the gas and sped down the street.

"Friend of yours?" I asked.

"It's a long story. She is one of the people I want you to investigate. Her name is Miko Tashima and she was the girlfriend of the late Roger Black. But let me start at the beginning. I am the leader of a group of spiritual aspirants. We are an esoteric cult and are held with disdain, or worse, by more traditional religious denominations.

"Three months ago, Roger Black, Miko's boyfriend, was killed in a hit-and-run accident. The car and the driver were never found. At first we rejoiced. He had left our congregation in a fury, threatening to report our church to the Internal Revenue Service for irregularities. But our joy was short lived.

"Less than a month ago one of our most faithful and most beneficent members, Richard Steed, was found crushed at the base of a cliff. He'd been walking his dog and had fallen to his death. The police decided it was accidental.

"We started getting death threats. Some of them seemed as if they might be coming from Miko. But other notes suggested that the two murders were only the beginning of a wave of killings, a wave that would end with the death of my sister and myself.

"The police are singularly uninterested in pursuing the cause of this chain of coincidences. I imagine they would be quite relieved to let the bodies continue to accumulate."

I interrupted him. I'm no fan of the police, but this portrayal seemed overly callous, even for me. "Oh, come on, Edward. Aren't you being the teensiest bit paranoid?"

He sighed. "I haven't told you the name of our religion. That may help explain my deductions about law enforcement's bias against us. Back in 1975 two sects broke away from our founding church. The two dissenting sects were the Temple of Set and the Fellowship of the Arising Night, of which I am the founding priest. Our mother church was, if you hadn't figured out by now, the Church of Satan."

I started collecting up the cards in front of me. "That's it. I'm done. Bye, bye Mr. Lucifer. The last thing I need right now is a satanic priest pushing me to go up against the police to catch a serial killer. Not my cup of tea." I pushed the envelope toward him. "Here's your money back. Thanks but no thanks."

Again no movement on his part. He ignored my rejection, and just looked at me with eyes that were the color of the Caribbean. An uncomfortably long silence was broken by the shrill song of a police siren in the distance. He asked, "Do I look familiar? Take off about a hundred pounds."

So it wasn't just his resemblance to Santa. I mentally liposuctioned his face. There was something there, something that made my stomach twist even before I figured out who he really was. I had just jumped out of the frying pan and into the sixth Circle of Hell.

"Edward, my ass. What the fuck are you doing here, Strephon?"

Strephon Ventnor was the twin brother of a woman who had loved me and destroyed my life. I'd met him twice in the late sixties. Today, I'd never recognize him. But I saw Veronique in the set of his chin, and the ridge of his cheekbone, and most of all in the azure of his eyes.

He smiled. I shivered. "I want to—or more precisely my sister and I want to—engage your services to help us bring an end to these killings."

10

Shit. She was still alive. My throat went dry and tight. My stomach wanted to toss the Thai chicken burrito I had for lunch. I was afraid to speak. So I just looked at him, trying to keep my face impassive.

Veronique had been like a Fury from Greek mythology. She had swept into my life, bringing ecstasy, tragedy, and despair. Thirty years later I still dreamed of her: sometimes in lust, sometimes in grief, sometimes in terror.

Edward paused and sighed. Then he went on, "A month ago I brought Veronique to California from Europe. She's assisting me in the administration of the church. We've received repeated warnings that we will be the next two victims. I have nowhere else to turn. Please help us."

Goddamn him. Goddamn him, and her. Goddamn him and her and the whole fucking mess. All I wanted was a simple life. A simple life, a few good friends, and a clean break from my past. And all I kept getting was this kind of shit.

Last year, I would have walked off, got on my motorcycle, and driven into the sunset. I'd have tossed my Warren Ritter ID cards into the bay as I drove over the Richmond–San Rafael Bridge.

But last year I hadn't fallen in love. Last year I hadn't become a surrogate father to a teenager. And last year I damn well hadn't become so fucking dependent on my therapist that I couldn't just split and start again. I missed last year big time!

Could I live with the knowledge that I had stood by while someone killed Mr. Ventnor/Hightower? Sure, no problem. Could I read about the murder of Veronique and just shrug it off? Shit. There's the rub. Probably not. No, definitely not. I was trapped. I never wanted to see her again, but I didn't want

II

her death on my conscience. I already had enough deaths on my plate because of her.

Okay, I'll be honest. My life had settled down. And I was getting a little bored with it. I relished my new dating relationship. I had a great time with my teenage "daughter." But it was a very safe life I was leading these days. I missed the kind of danger that leaves your throat dry and makes you afraid that you're going to piss in your pants.

My voice came out raspy. "What do you want?"

He took a second, thicker envelope out of his pocket.

CHAPTER THREE

Denny's restaurant in Emeryville never closes. At four in the afternoon there was the usual international sprinkle of brown, yellow, and black families dining as cheaply as they could. Scattered among them was a bent old guy nursing a hot chocolate, three junkie girlfriends (twenty-five going on sixty), and a woman sitting alone at the counter, finishing her third cup of coffee. She had that "Stay the fuck away from me!" air about her. Nobody but the guy behind the counter had said a word to her. The woman was scribbling relentlessly in a red journal. Occasionally, she would consult a book that lay open next to her. Then she would go back to writing.

This is the tale of a dangerous woman. There is a small cadre of people in the world who are more than just human beings. Most of their work is done in the darkness, and their accomplishments are usually never discovered. If they are unmasked, their deeds are branded as insanity or criminality. The only ones to achieve any lasting notoriety are the men. If something should happen to me, the world needs to know the power that a woman can wield. If you're reading this, know that women are to be feared!

I live above the rules. Commandments, doctrines, injunctions, and laws no longer apply to me. You God-fearing Christians, righteous Muslims, neurotic Jews, or immobile Buddhists go ahead, continue to worship your chains. Ignore the murder you all have already committed. Freddie Nietzche has already exposed your crime and spoken your sentence. I love him for this. His judgment has set me free.

> "Where has God gone?" he cried. "I shall tell you. We have killed him—you and I. We are his murderers. But how have we done this? How were we able to drink up the sea? Who gave us the sponge to wipe away the entire horizon? What did we do when we unchained the earth from its sun? Whither is it moving now? Whither are we moving now? Away from all suns? Are we not perpetually falling? . . . God is dead. God remains dead. And we have killed him. How shall we, murderers of all murderers, console ourselves? . . . Must we not ourselves become gods simply to be worthy of it? There has never been a greater deed; and whosoever shall be born after us—for the sake of this deed he shall be part of a higher history than all history hitherto."

Not rage, not vengeance, although rage and vengeance are sweet. What drives me transcends such petty motivations. I do what I do simply because I can. I take what I need, and if blood must be spilt, so be it.

The time of lightning and thunder has come. The deeds are being accomplished, one life at a time. The plan is simple. Spread out the noose, and then tighten it until only two are left standing. Then let the trapdoor drop open.

She was working. She liked planning the jobs in restaurants. Everyone else was thinking about whether to order a burger, or to be good and get the chicken Caesar salad. She was deciding how to end a life.

She was stuck right now, but she knew inspiration would come. After all, God helps those who help themselves.

CHAPTER FOUR

I watched Hightower (aka Ventnor, Beelzebub, and who knew what else) waddle away from my table and meld into the Telegraph rabble. This experience sucked. I was so done for the day. Maybe for the decade. I packed up my cards, folded the table, and grabbed my sign. I took everything into Cody's, the big local bookstore in front of the stretch of sidewalk that I called my office. I walked though the STAFF ONLY door and dropped everything but my cards in the corner of the back storeroom. I rented that corner for a pittance, plus an occasional free tarot card reading for a member of the bookstore staff.

I needed a good stiff drink. But drinking while on my medication could have unpredictable effects. Fun sometimes, but definitely unpredictable. Not what I needed right now.

I wanted a session with my therapist. I thought about calling her and getting an emergency appointment. But I stopped myself. This was no emergency, just scary and chaotic. I could wait untill my regular appointment Wednesday night.

That left my girlfriend. Well, my girlfriends, actually. I mean one of them was my friend, who happened to be a girl. Heather was a real girl, just turned seventeen. The other one was "girl-friend" in the romantic sense of that word. Sally was in her mid-thirties, a wheelchair-driving basketball star, and a hacker of international renown. They lived together on a small ranch out in the grassy hills behind the East Bay. I had to call first to see if they were receiving gentlemen callers. Come in unannounced and Sally's attack-trained Rottweiler would flatten me.

"How 'ex' a girlfriend?" Sally went straight to the most uncomfortable part of my tale.

"Thirty years ex. I can hardly remember what she looked like. Besides, she liked girls better than boys."

We were sitting in front of a stone fireplace. It was just starting to cast a rosy light into the room. Heather and I each had our own overstuffed leather chairs, while Sally sat in her titanium racing chair. I put part of my attention on the story of my bizarre encounter with Edward. The rest of me was enjoying the yellow-orange light of the fire as it theatrically lit those two very good-looking women.

Sally McLaughlin was a runaway nuclear reaction enclosed in a taut, strong, female body. After the accident that crushed her spine and ended her Army career, she took up programming with vengeance in mind. After succeeding magnificently at paying back the driver and his commanding officer for their neglect, she'd gone on to hack into databases all over the world. She amassed gigabytes of sensitive information about governments, corporations, churches, police departments, and anything else that captured her fancy. She contracted her services out to individuals and organizations that shared her political beliefs, which were a little to the left of Trotsky.

But the most amazing thing about Sally was her smile. When it was turned on you, a warm, full, buttery glow began to spread from somewhere deep inside your abdomen. All of a sudden you remembered summers at the lake, kittens falling asleep in tight furry balls, and that birthday present you never dared to put on your wish list. I'm manic-depressive. I don't get how someone can smile like that so often. The first time I saw it, I was hooked. I couldn't stay away from it.

Sometimes that smile warmed up other parts of my anatomy. Sally was electric when she turned on the juice. We were in the savoring phase, still not boiling over in the consummation of full lovers, but keeping a lively simmer going: fueled by flames of physical and emotional foreplay.

Sally and I were "going out," a quaint custom for a guy over fifty. What it meant, in locker-room parlance, is that we were somewhere between second and third base. So far, I hadn't stayed the night. Sally wasn't positive that I might not run away if things got tough, and she wasn't willing to throw her heart over the fence unless she knew that she could trust me.

This was a reasonable caution to take. I'd been on the run since 1970. During that time I had established three separate identities in three states—each of which paid income tax, had a driver's license, and maintained a legal residence. I almost disappeared from Berkeley earlier this year when I was afraid that my Warren Ritter identity was about to get torn apart. Hell, I wasn't too sure if I could tough out the really hard times. Running's an addiction. But I was here now, giving it my best.

Heather wrinkled her forehead, managing to look curious and cute at the same time. "I don't get it. What's this Hightower guy have on you that would make you work for him?"

Heather Talbridge (she had changed her name back from Wellington after her hated stepfather had died) was just coming into the delectableness of womanhood: that age Madison Avenue has decided is the pinnacle of feminine splendor. Actually, to fit with Madison Ave's anorectic ideal, she would have to lose fifty pounds. As a haunted skeleton she'd be perfect for *Vogue*. Instead she was brimming over with life. Eros, curiosity, and bitchiness lit up her green eyes. The last was a character trait easily forgiven in a beautiful woman.

Heather had no parents, and was independently wealthy: every teenager's dream. She got herself declared an emancipated minor by the courts. She adopted Sally as a mentor to live with and to help launch her into adulthood.

Sally's influence was bearing fruit. Heather no longer wore her mahogany hair in spikes. She'd let it grow so that it curled down around her long neck. Streaked auburn highlights caught the firelight.

I'd only hinted at my debased past to Heather. Now it was time to come partially clean. "I was involved with a group of war resisters and we got in trouble with the law. I went underground and cut ties with that group. Edward knew me back then, and his sister was in the group with me. If he exposes me I could be arrested for what I did back in those days."

"So you're still living underground?"

I nodded.

"Your name's not really Warren Ritter?"

I nodded again.

"What is it?"

Oh, shit. Why does that name keep coming back into my conversations? I considered brushing her off. But Heather had been through some rough times. She had every reason in the world to distrust men. I felt I had to come clean.

"Look, I don't tell anyone this. The two of you are very important to me. Please promise not to say this name to anyone. And Sally, you especially, please promise not to research me."

Heather said, "Sure."

Sally was quiet for a moment. "Warren, I appreciate you starting to let us in. I don't know what happened to you, and I promise that I won't pry. But I do know that you and I need to have all that history out on the table sometime soon."

God, I hate being busted. "I know that too, Sally. And I'm going to tell you everything, very soon. It's just hard, after keeping this secret for so long. Anyway, here is chapter one. My name is . . . was Richard Green. During the sixties and early seventies I was in an organization called the Weather Underground."

Heather asked, "And thirty years later you're hiding from the police?"

"Yes."

"Is that why you still keep my mom's old cell phone, but you want me to pay the bill for it?"

I'd known I was going to have to explain that someday. "Yep. I keep it in my flight bag in case I have to go into hiding." I hated talking about this. It confused Heather and worried Sally. Sally was always waiting for me to climb on my motorcycle and run away from her, from Berkeley, and from "the full catastrophe" as Zorba put it.

Heather wrinkled her forehead. "You were a terrorist?"

21

I sighed. "Heather, life was a little more complex back then. These days someone is either a terrorist or a good guy. When I was your age—oh, that sounds awful. I have become an old fart. Let's say, back in the sixties it wasn't the fanatical Arab terrorists versus the red, white, and blue. It was the cops and the National Guard against the blacks and the kids."

"I'm not naive." She impatiently brushed a strand of hair back from her face. "Life hasn't changed much. Go to any high school and you learn in a big hurry about violent cops."

"I apologize. You know what I'm talking about." Her boyfriend was black. He had instantly become a suspect when she'd been kidnapped, primarily because of his race.

But I couldn't just let it end there. There's one big difference between the time I was growing up and your world, Heather. Society ignores you, but it doesn't hate you. When I was a little older than you my hair was down to my shoulders. When I walked down the street, I never knew if a car full of rednecks or Marines on leave from Vietnam would pull over, start yelling, "Long-haired, hippie, nigger-loving commie!" and beat the shit out of me. It happened more than once.

"If I was walking arm in arm with a black girl I could almost guarantee that I was going to get trashed. It could be worse though. If I'd been a black guy walking with a white girl I would have stood a good chance of getting shot. And no two guys could ever walk hand in hand.

"When longhairs got beaten, the police did nothing, except to make damn sure I knew they sided with the attackers. A lot of the folks in my generation felt the country was out to get us."

There was a long pause after that outburst. Finally Sally said, "Warren, I want to get back to the story about Hightower. Are

22

you going to need any help from me with this escapade?"

She was right. I'd been on my soapbox. "I'm sorry, Heather. I used to hate it when my father gave long speeches about Communists at the dinner table. I don't want to be like that."

Heather giggled. "It's okay. You're cute when you get riled up."

Sally's interruption and Heather's laugh disconcerted me. I sat back in my chair, reluctant to jump into business. The end of one of the logs in the fireplace broke off and created a fire fall of glowing coals. I watched how the light caught the red in Heather's hair, warmed up the red leather of our chairs, and glittered off the red burgundy in the wineglasses that the two women held. My Diet Coke didn't reflect much.

I turned to Sally. "Yes, I need your help desperately." I handed her the thick envelope Edward had given me. ENEMIES OF THE CHURCH was written on it in an angular, precise hand. "Here are the most violent hate letters and e-mails that Edward's received in the past four months. None of them are explicit enough for the police to regard as evidence, but this may be a good place to start. I need whatever information you can find out about whoever sent them."

Then I handed her a single sheet with my handwriting on it. "Here is the name of another person out to get Edward: Miko Tashima—a girlfriend of one of the victims. I wrote down the license number of her car. Tell me what you can find out about her, too."

"This is business, Warren. It's going to cost you."

She was the best there was at data snatching. "I want this over as fast as I can. Go ahead and do what you have to. Edward's footing the bill, so don't let money stop you."

23

She smiled. Oh, that smile! "Okay, boss man. I'll e-mail you public record stuff tomorrow. Look for subject line 'Groovy Stuff.' The other material will be put on the big table inside your apartment's foyer in a manila envelope marked 'Subscription Services.' It should be coming in Thursday".

How did she know about that table? This woman never ceased to disconcert me.

Sally went on, "Let's roll the tape back, Warren. I have a question about what you were talking about before."

"Shoot."

"What did you do that was so bad you had to disappear?"

I panicked. I wasn't ready. "Look, that has to do with the secret. I have to practice first with my therapist. I'll tell Rose. Then I'll tell you, both of you. But not yet."

Sally nodded. "Just don't get yourself killed in the meantime. Whenever you go investigating, someone ends up shooting at you. Stay alive, okay? Two inquiring minds want to know your mystery of mysteries."

"I'll make sure I stay alive."

I bent down and gave Sally a long kiss, one that made me want to abandon my plans to drive home. I finally broke free, and gave Ripley, Sally's Rottweiler attack dog, a scratch behind the ears. Ripley looked up adoringly. I was under no illusions. One command from Sally and she would go for my throat. But until then she would stretch her neck to help me get to a particularly itchy spot.

Heather walked me out to my car. The crescent moon hung silver in the black sky. The smell of cut grass mingled with a hint of the sweet odor from petroleum refineries, creating a fragrance that was not unpleasant.

24

Heather said, "Thanks for tonight, Warren. I read about the Vietnam War and the protestors. But I never thought about it much. Mostly, the sixties are just Beatles songs and Austin Powers movies. I didn't realize it was so scary. I do want to know more about that part of your life, and about who you really are. I care about you, Warren. You're the closest thing to a dad that I've got."

I gave her a hug, so she couldn't see my eyes well up. Then I hurried away.

CHAPTER FIVE

As far as she was concerned, variety was the spice of life. Or of death. Only two obstacles stood between her and final retribution. She wanted to eliminate them with a little élan.

Poison could work this time, quite nicely. But it had to look accidental enough so that the police could follow their natural reluctance to investigate further. This was a challenge!

She went to Borders, a big impersonal bookstore where no one would remember her. There she discovered *Deadly Doses: A Writer's Guide to Poisons*. Delightful reading. She found what she wanted: It was a nut that grew in tropical climates. It was addictively delicious, deadly toxic, and it killed in less than an hour. She knew just the slimeball expat who would be able to get his hands on some.

She was not yet finished. Ending the victim's life was just a matter of a quick flight to Mexico City, looking up Tony, and then making a hot fudge sundae with extra nuts. But for this death to look accidental, that was the challenge!

She sat in the café at the bookstore, gracefully tearing off tiny pieces of her croissant, dipping them in her Earl Gray tea, and placing them gently in her mouth. Her eyes glazed as she stared out the window. Then she had it. She said out loud, "Cherubim." The image that came into her mind was not the cute little toddler with wings who graced Valentine cards. She saw the Old Testament guardians of the Tree of Life, holding flaming swords above their heads.

Perfect. She smiled and brushed a flake from her lips with her napkin. Now she knew which victim to select, where the crime would occur, and how. She pulled out her journal and began to make a "to do" list. She was going to be very busy this week.

CHAPTER SIX

L abor Day, the first Monday in September; it shouldn't be a holiday, it should be a wake. The international megacorporations have gutted the labor movement. These days the holiday is celebrated by running down to the big sale at Target to stock up on designer jeans stitched together by children working twelve hours a day in Southeast Asia.

I imagined asking any of the kids who were cruising past me, "Hey, what do you know about the labor movement in this country?" They'd stare blankly at me. Maybe they'd say, "You mean like being pregnant and in labor?" or "That happened sometime in the fifties, didn't it?"

They would not have a clue about what this holiday signified. Conservative American history textbook writers have written the unions out of the public school curriculum. Angry progressive politics don't fit with their cartoon stereotype of the "melting pot of the free and the home of the brave."

A teacher wouldn't dare mention the Memorial Day

massacre (ten strikers killed by police), the Lattimer Mine incident (nineteen strikers shot in the back by a posse), or the Ludlow massacre where Rockefeller's guards fired machine guns into a union strikers' tent camp killing five men, two women, and twelve children. The school board would fire her, or him, in a minute for being Un-American.

These kids don't know that Joe Hill was framed and hanged in spite of attempts by the president of the United States to stop the execution. And they don't care. They might have heard the song on a geezer rock 'n' roll station, and that's about it. Over four hundred Americans have been shot or lynched by police or militia while protesting unfair working conditions. Except for good old Joe Hill, they all died unsung and in vain. Happy Labor Day!

It was damn hot. After the first week of firestorm weather you start bickering with anyone who gets within fifteen feet of you. After a month of desiccating, incessant wind you seriously think about ramming that BMW in front of you. By now it had been over six weeks. The place felt like Phoenix. I wanted to find a lowlife bar and start a brawl.

I was working Telegraph because I thought I might make a few extra bucks on the holiday. But once I set up shop I regretted it. I sat at my table and watched tourists waste their money. There was no hope for them. They weren't worth my time. I began to wonder if it might be time to increase my antidepressants.

Labor Day, bah, humbug! I decided to close early. As I was gathering up my cards and crystal paperweights someone slung a leg of mutton over my shoulder. No; it was just a hand. An extremely heavy hand.

"You've been showing up in my cards, Warren."

Philip Letour was my tarot card mentor. Decades ago he'd scared the shit out of me when he psychically nailed me. It was my first encounter with tarot cards. Earlier this year he had come back into my life, and, in another reading, he pointed me toward a murderer. He was the only guy I knew who actually could read the future from these damn cards. Which is impossible. I know that, in my rational mind. But he'd done it enough times to make me very nervous around him.

As a psychic, I'm a bit of an imposter. I regard tarot card reading as an activity that falls on the leisure-time continuum somewhere between television and therapy. It's a cheap form of entertainment and a nice soothing panacea for the part of us that hungers to have an expert tell us that everything is going to work out all right. But it ain't real. We're all posers.

Except for Philip. Everything he ever told me came to pass, whether I understood it at the time or not. So I hated it when he told me I was showing up in his cards. I really didn't want to know that I was about to die or something worse. Like ending up in jail.

But he wasn't the kind of guy you could just tell to buzz off. He was the biggest man I had ever met. Kind of a movable mountain range of a man: over six feet tall, with a shiny, bald head, burnt-chocolate predator eyes, and long, deeply lined, dexterous fingers. All the rest was bulk.

His voice was very deep and he spoke with a slight Southern accent. "I thought I'd come over here and look you up. There's some rough water ahead."

I'd learned not to waste time with Philip. He never stayed for long. "Good to see you, Philip. Why do you always show up whenever I have another murderer to catch? Don't bother

31

answering that. I don't think I want to know. Anyway, I'm after a guy who is knocking off . . ." It finally sunk in what he'd said. "What did you mean, 'rough waters'?"

He took a red silk bag out of his inside breast pocket. He carefully removed a deck of ancient, oversized, Italian tarot cards, and began to gently cut and re-cut the deck. Then he spread the cards out in a line facedown across my table. "I'll show you what I mean. Choose four cards."

He turned over the first of my chosen cards. A tall red tower had just been struck by lightning. The ornate balconies and cornices on the upper structure were tipping over, and two figures, a man in a tunic and a woman in a red flowing dress were falling to their death.

Philip said, "Ah, the Tower. Three decades ago you turned over this card. Then, you fled from my studio. You were not yet ready to face your past. This time there's no running away. The past holds the key to your future. If you try to flee, you will be destroyed." See why I like this guy?

Then he turned over the next card—a woman in a white cloak sitting on a throne wearing a tiara. She wore three more crowns above that. Hum, interesting. "The Popess. A woman pope was considered heretical. This card was dropped from many tarot decks in the fifteenth and sixteenth centuries. The church burned heretics who thought that a woman could become a priest or a pope. Owning this card could have gotten you killed. In your modern decks she is called the High Priestess. This woman may be a stranger to you right now, or a close friend, but she is the person who will bring the Tower down."

The third card depicted a beggar in a tunic, codpiece, and boots, but wearing no pants. He had white feathers stuck in his

hair and was juggling three white balls. He appeared to be unaware that he was about to step off a cliff.

Philip gently tapped the card and said, "Here's the reason I
came to see you. This is your card, and in the past week he's
been wandering through my spreads with alarming regularity."

"What makes it my card?"

"I don't know. I just know I think of you whenever he
shows up. What do you know of tarocchi, the game these cards
were designed for?"

It was hot. I was grumpy. I hadn't asked for this meeting. So
I cut funky. "Oh, you mean tarot cards aren't the distillation of
the esoteric teachings contained in the library of Alexander,
spirited away by gypsies, and hidden from religious zealots for
centuries?"

"Very funny." He didn't look amused. "You know damn
well that story was nothing but nineteenth-century theosophi-
cal horseshit. I'm speaking here of the true history. Tarocchi was
a game started in the late 1400s—a little like bridge, but with a
whole lot of trump cards.

Now, "the Fool is one of those trumps. It's the weakest card
in the deck, and yet one of the most valuable. It gives you more
points than a king, and yet it is powerless to take any other card.
And that, Warren, will be your dilemma: valuable and powerless.
Your value will not lie in what you do, which will ultimately be
ineffectual."

This was not helping. "Oh, thanks a lot. So where does my
value lie?"

He shrugged. "Dammed if I know. You'll have to find that
out."

"You're a real pal, Philip."

He turned over the final card. It depicted a woman in the center of a circle. A hopeful page was climbing up on the left side of the circle, a happy king sat on the throne above her, a frightened man was falling headfirst down to the right margin, and a weary, broken old man crawled at her feet, the circle resting on his bent back.

Philip said, "Ah, the Wheel of Fortune." Then he started to sing. *Fortune rota volvitur: descendo minoratus; alter in altum tollitur nimis exaltatus; rex sedet in vertice—caveat ruinam!* But your Latin is probably a little rusty.

"It translates something like, 'The Wheel of Fortune turns. I go down, demeaned. Another is raised up. Far too proud sits the king at the summit—let him fear ruin!' Those medieval monks are speaking directly to you, Warren. You must lose everything, and the king must fall before this drama ends." He gathered up his cards and put them back in his pocket.

"Gee, thanks for dropping by with the good news, Philip. Come back again real soon."

"Warren, there's also some good news in that last card. While it is true that the Wheel will turn for you, it will also turn for your adversaries. Do not ever lose hope."

He weighed anchor and pulled away from my table and into the sea of pedestrians streaming past. Soon only the bright top of his head was visible.

I must lose everything? That didn't sound like much fun.

CHAPTER SEVEN

Tuesday greeted me with the bells playing upbeat renditions of Beatles songs, the sun sparkling through the windows, and the birds chirping merrily. I wanted to fly an airplane into the bell tower.

Instead, I went to clean the bathroom. On my hands and knees reaching around in back of the toilet, I reflected on the merciless cruelty of a God who could create such saccharine cheerfulness outside, and such claustrophobic gloom in my psyche. Job had nothing on me. I really must have offended Jehovah in a previous lifetime.

Desperate times require desperate measures. I walked across the street and got two maple bars and a huge cup of vanilla-flavored coffee at the doughnut shop. The coffee was only a few grades above transmission fluid. However, the chemical interaction of fried dough, artificial maple flavoring, and caffeine creates a well-known folk remedy for depression. It's also a good cure for anorexia.

Thus fortified and bloated, I decided what the hell, since everything is stale, flat, and unprofitable, I might as well sleuth. I sat down with Microsoft Publisher and printed up a phony business card and a press ID. Then I called Sally.

"Hey, I was just getting ready to mail you some stuff," she said. "This is turning out to be a lot more fun than I thought it would. Anyway, where do you want to start?"

"Fun?"

"Uh-oh, sounds like the blues are busting somebody's balls in Berkeley."

"Fun, right. Well, tell me about your fun."

"The gal in the Z-3 is today's project."

"Girl. Yeah, that's a good place to start."

Sally gave me the scoop on Miko's addresses (in Berkeley and in Kyoto, Japan), student status (two-year international transfer from Kyoto University, the Department of Human Coexistence), Kyoto school colors (navy blue, same as the BMW she purchased for cash three months ago), and recent purchases (Colt Python Elite .357 magnum revolver).

"Warren, please be careful. These killings have been committed by someone who is very pissed off, and very good at killing people. Don't get too close, okay?"

"No problem, Sally. I have it all under control."

I tracked Miko to her lair, an upper-floor flat in the prestigious north side of Berkeley. The house was a white Victorian that must have just missed being torched in the Great Fire of '23. A Queen Anne with curved bay windows, a wide side porch, and a sweeping circular balcony held up by four classic columns. Nice digs for a student. Hell, nice digs for a professor.

I pushed the bell at 376B Oxford Street. I watched through the glass panel in the front door as a young Asian woman I didn't recognize came skipping down the stairs. "May I help you?"

"Yes. I'm looking for Miko Tashima. I understand that she lives here."

"One moment."

She bounced back up the stairs calling Miko's name, saying something in Japanese, and giggling. I tried not to take it personally. Then the lady in the Z-3 came down to investigate.

"Hello, Ms. Tashima. My name's Warren Ritter, and I'm writing an article for *The Express* about the Fellowship of the Arising Night. I understand that a friend of yours, Mr. Roger Black, was a disgruntled ex-member. I am sorry about his death. I wanted to know if you could help me get his story told." I held out my freshly minted card.

She took it, but barely glanced at it. "Come on up, Mr. Ritter. I have quite a lot to tell you."

She led me into the sunny front living room, with a lovely view of the Berkeley Hills. I settled into the fawn-colored leather couch and accepted a Diet Coke on ice. Miko was attractive in an anime/*Tank Girl* sort of way, with short spiked hair, intense brown eyes, broad shoulders, and strong forearms. She looked like a martial artist, not like a sweet young thing. She had no accent, unless you call a Southern California slur an accent. She perched on a Second Empire settee upholstered in gold brocade and began the interrogation.

"What kind of article are you writing?"

"Well, I've heard rumors of financial mismanagement and brainwashing, and I wanted to check them out. Also it seems to

37

me the death of Mr. Black was awfully convenient for the church."

She pointed at me. "Don't call it a church. It's a cult, plain and simple. Thank God someone is finally investigating this. That Hightower asshole and his slut sister are murderers. Roger was murdered. He was young, strong, and had great reflexes. So I don't think it was a car accident. It was deliberate, and damn well-planned. They never found the driver or the car. I know he was killed to keep him silent."

I nodded and asked, "How do you know?"

She took a big breath. "Roger worked with Ella Fletcher, the bitch who handles the blood money for the cult. He started noticing things like Hightower's six-figure salary and other irregularities. When he brought it up he was drummed out of the cult. He was looking for a reporter like you to help him expose what was going on. Then he got assassinated. The morning he was killed he called me and told me he had all he needed to blow that place apart."

"What did he have?"

"He didn't tell me. We never got the chance to meet and talk about it. I had to go to class, so I cut him off. That was the last time we spoke. I'm going to make every one of those demons pay!"

She occilated between guilt and vengeance. A little scary. I kept acting like Clark Kent, star reporter. "Did he leave any evidence behind?"

A woman's voice came up the stairway. "Mitsue, Miko, wassup girls?"

Miko's roommate yelled out, "Leticia, come on up."

Shit! I looked over and saw one of my regular tarot card

customers coming up the stairs. I was in deep doo-doo.

She got to the landing and looked in. "Yo, Warren, how's your bones?" Then to Miko she said, "Priestess, you getting your cards done?"

Miko furrowed her brows. "Cards? What do you mean, 'Tish?"

Leticia was six feet tall and weighed in the high two hundreds. She was very black and dressed in a flowing African print dress. She swept into the living room. "Mr. Warren Ritter here is the best damn tarot card reader in California, that's all."

Miko looked more closely at me, and her eyes widened. "You! I remember you. You were on Telegraph last Sunday. You were with him. You were talking with that Hightower fiend. You're not a reporter. What the fuck is going on here?"

I knew I should have stayed on the floor of my bathroom, cleaning the grout. "I'm investigating your boyfriend's death."

"Oh yeah? With what, tea leaves? And who's paying you?"

It was time to go now. I got up and walked toward the stairs, hoping Miko wouldn't plug me with her brand-new .357 in front of so many witnesses. Miko began shouting at me. She threw my fake business card at my retreating back.

Her roommate came in to watch the show. She must have enjoyed it because she smiled and waved good-bye as I passed her and walked down the stairs.

I heard Mitsue exclaim as I dropped out of sight, "You will pay for lying to me, Warren Ritter!"

These kinds of things never happened to Travis Magee.

CHAPTER EIGHT

I slunk home. As I entered my apartment, I heard my cell phone announce from the dining room table that my voicemail was bursting with tidings of great joy. It turned out to be my new employer.

Edward said, "Warren, I would like to take my afternoon constitutional with you today. We have some important things to discuss. Call me and let me know if you can make it."

I figured this was a sign from heaven. God obviously set this up so that I could tell Mr. Hightower that I stink as a PI. Then I could quit. I called and agreed to meet him in an hour at the Albany Bulb.

For decades the residents of the East Bay had been dumping their solid waste into a landfill along the edge of the bay. Finally someone noticed that the fish were dying and that the most scenic stretches of the East Bay shoreline were devoted to garbage. The dumps were closed.

The existing landfills were unusable, unsafe, and therefore ignored by developers and city planners. One of these areas was called the Bulb, an oval protuberance connected to the mainland by a narrow neck of land, wide enough for two dump trucks to pass each other. Fennel and pampas grass had begun to cover the rebar and chunks of concrete that were the Cypress Freeway Structure, before the '89 quake leveled it.

First the homeless found it, a haven tucked behind the huge Albany Racetrack and unpatrolled by police. Then something mad and miraculous happened. Artists started using the concrete slabs as vast canvasses for their work. Sculptors fashioned statues and giant archways from found bricks and debris washed ashore from passing freighters. A bust made out of bits of shell and glass looked across a dirt trail at a mural of a goddess copulating with a giant squid. A castle emerged, built of slabs of plywood, and circled by a rickety staircase. The interior walls of a concrete tunnel became a wraparound mural. One walked and crawled through this chaotic, postmodern temple, continually delighted by surrealistic images of the decay of the American Empire.

Such primitive, explicit unveiling of the dark side of modern society could not be allowed to continue. The town of Albany was a haven of respectability. It prided itself on its tree-lined streets, excellent school scores, and upper-middle-class homogeneity. The Bulb, a dark, passionate snake eating away at the roots of Albany's edifice of decorum, had to be eviscerated.

A coalition of concerned citizens, regional parks experts, governmental agencies, and cops managed to leash the dogs and exile the homeless. They wanted to destroy the art, too, but it's hard to toss out painted hunks of concrete. Dynamite was suggested as a solution.

Edward wore extra-large, dark green shorts and hiking boots

made from heavy brown leather. His short-sleeved yellow polo shirt was not tucked in. He was ready for the scramble.

We headed out beyond the sedate "Urban Promenade" clogged with yuppies jogging with their three-wheeled perambulators or trying to keep up to their purebred dogs Soon the pavement ends and the ruts begin. You crawl around twisted metal and slide down concrete slopes to get to the art museum. On the way down we came upon a smoking campfire surrounded by seven twisted-wire sculptures the size of humans, ornamented with ribbons, glass pendulums, and other flashy found objects. It was Calder's Boy Scout troop.

We sat on a log beside the fire. I was waiting for his opening move. Finally Edward said, "I painted some of my poetry on concrete out here. I'll show it to you on our way out. It was the only way I could get published."

Another pause. Then, "Warren. I've got an apology to make. My sister browbeat me to take you on as our rescuer. I never liked the idea."

What did he want? "Don't the means justify the ends? That sounds like a moral tenet satanists would espouse. If you have moral tenets."

Edward gave me that Santa smile. "You don't know squat about my religion, Warren. Before all this ends we'll have to rectify that. We do believe in morality, in our way. We believe that no moral code can be imposed from outside. But that does not mean we espouse rape, pillage, and murder. Each of us has an innate sense of right and wrong, once you can just get all the bullshit commandments and injunctions out of the way."

He got up. "Enough of the sermon. Come with me and I'll show you my 'published work.'"

We climbed down to the shoreline. In silence we walked past the wall of plywood murals done by a five-artist collective known as Sniff. We walked through an arch held up on either side by giant sculptures, one a disgusted woman and the other a wimpy man. This structure was made up of planks, metal, and chunks of discarded Styrofoam flotation material. We passed the rotting hulls of several pleasure boats grounded and deserted on the rocky banks. Again Edward began to climb, and we found a ramshackle bench overlooking the bay. It was the only place in fifty square miles that had a cool breeze. Nearby was a face of concrete with two haiku painted on it.

> *Sold the house,*
> *closed the cabin,*
> *I am moving into the empty room.*

> *Night sky beckons me.*
> *My words and I fade away . . .*
> *gone without a trace.*

I said, "You don't sound like a satanist, you sound like a Zen Buddhist. Where's the fire and brimstone?"

He smiled. "Our faith is more about darkness than it is about fire. We believe that you find the truth by turning away from the light. The harsh glare of righteousness blinds people into believing that they are the carriers of the truth. Nothing is true in darkness. That's why it's my friend. I've always loved the darkness. It saved my life more than once over in 'Nam, and it continues to guide me."

I said, "Vietnam? God, knowing your sister it's hard to believe you went over there."

He looked out over the flat water and said softly, "I'm a bit more lawful than Veronique. In '70, when Nixon pulled all the deferments, I'd already lost the draft lottery. I didn't want to become an expatriate, so I went. I was a Red Devil (appropriate, don't you think?): Fifth Infantry Mechanized. We worked the Khe Sanh area in Laos. Ran out of bullets, froze our asses off. Kids in camouflage and kids in black pajamas killing each other. Just as we were pulling out, I took a piece of shrapnel big enough to send me home."

He shook himself. "I want to get back to our contractual relationship. Actually, I want to release you from our agreement. It's not right to get drafted, no matter who does it. If you want to help us you can, but if you want to walk away I'm not going to fuck with you."

He'd outmaneuvered me. Now I really had to choose, not just react to someone else's power trip. My first thought was to shake his hand and walk off. I could leave Edward the satanist in a flash, no problem. But, Edward the poet, the vet, the outcast philosopher—damn, he'd gotten to me.

Some of us guys who dodged the draft or rode out the war stateside in the Air National Guard harbor an unspoken guilt. We usually don't think about it. But it lurks there, waiting. The kid down the block went over. Maybe he came back in a box or in a wheelchair. Maybe he looked fine on the outside. But he hits his wife, walks off his job, drinks beyond reason, or just wakes up in the middle of the night screaming. He was scarred. Some of those wounds don't heal. And he took those wounds in my place.

45

So, I spoke out of guilt, respect. and a feeling that we were not so far apart. I decided that if I had any say about it, I wasn't going to let anyone kill this guy. I said, "Count me in. I still think you need the police investigating all this. If you want me, I'll see this one through."

He said, "You were a mensch back in '70 when you did the hard thing in New York, and you're a mensch still. Thanks, War-ren. We need you."

CHAPTER NINE

ose, I need your help as a forensic consultant, not as my therapist. I need you to profile a killer."

"It'll cost you."

It was Wednesday night, and I was sitting in the living room/office of my therapist, Rose Janeworth. Rose lived just north of Berkeley, in a tiny village called Kensington. Actually Kensington looked like Brigadoon splattered up against a hillside. Quaint brown-shingled cottages lined winding streets; wisteria hung down over garden trellises. It was all just too quaint.

A stone walkway led around the side of the house to her therapy office. It was the living room of her house and had a breathtaking view of the bay. The sun resisted setting. It hung over the Golden Gate Bridge, glaring into the room.

"Okay, how much extra is this going to cost me?"

She smiled. It was not a Mommy-loves-you smile. More like a feline you-look-good-enough-to-eat smile. "This is not about money, Warren. You've been dragging some horrible secret along with you for thirty years. I don't know what you did and I don't care what you did. But I want you to drop your load. Tell me what set you on the run back in the sixties and then I'll consult with you."

I hate Rose. I hate her because she's always digging, always trying to twist my secrets out of me.

I would have bailed out on her a long time ago, like I did with every other snoopy therapist I ever met. Only she was different from them. Early on she told me a story about her criminal past, a story that I could use to have her license taken away. No therapist had ever taken a risk like that with me before. I was pretty sure that she genuinely cared about my sorry ass. So I kept coming back.

Rose was in her seventies, maybe. But she was no matron. She was trim, and always stylishly dressed. Tonight she wore a lilac pantsuit that had dark purple irises embroidered into the velvet. Her gray hair fell long across her shoulders. Her blue eyes glittered like sapphires as the light began to turn golden in the room. The emerald in the gold necklace she always wore caught a ray of the sunset and bounced it back into my eyes, like a green laser beam.

I put on my tough-guy mask. "Ha, ha, Rose, I was going to do that anyway. But I want a renegotiation. We consult first, then I spill my guts. Otherwise no deal."

She nodded. "My therapist hat is off, and my consultant's cap is on. What's your problem?"

I told her about Hightower and his nemesis. I called the unknown serial killer the Satan Slayer. I finished up, "So the cops might be secretly cheering him on. How can I catch this guy?"

Rose leaned forward. "I need to do some education with you first before we get around to profiling our suspect. Assuming that these deaths are not coincidences, your killer easily falls within the genus of sociopath. That would mean we're looking for someone who is amoral, egocentric, stimulus seeking, and perhaps impulsive. A majority of them never run afoul of the law. Often they are successful businessmen or politicians who are not bothered by pesky ethical concerns. It's rarer than you imagine. Sociopaths constitute only three percent of the general male population and less than one percent of the female population.

"Mostly concentrated in Washington?" I asked.

She ignored me. "We can divide this group up, too. The common sociopath is a person who enjoys breaking the rules. They tend to be lusty risk takers. The alienated sociopath is cold and withdrawn; he or she just doesn't care about others. The dyssocial sociopath is the loyal member of a lawless gang. Finally, the aggressive sociopath enjoys hurting people.

"Male serial killers usually come from this last group. And they are pretty rare. Less than two percent of murders could fit into the definition of a serial killing. You know, Warren, as I think about it there's something about these murders that doesn't seem to fit the picture. I wonder if we aren't on the wrong trail altogether."

Great. She was stymied, too. "So, what are they, acts of God?"

She sighed and just looked at me for a moment. Maybe a little exasperated? Then she went on, "We've got two crimes with no clues. Neither involves torture. They both are linked with letters claiming that they are acts of vengeance. They might be done for profit, or for revenge. But they aren't violent, brutal, sexually oriented, or random. I don't think we have a serial killer here. We might just have a killer."

"Earlier you said 'male serial killers.' I thought almost all serial killers were male."

"Think again. Sixteen percent of serial killers are female and that number is rising. Actually these crimes might fit the profile of a woman killer. Men serials usually have some weird psycho-sexual component to their murders. Women who kill more than two people usually do it out of a desire for money, control, or revenge. They often know the people they kill, unlike most men serial killers who choose random victims.

"Your killings were relatively clean, well thought out, and subtle. The mark of a woman. But one thing about the killings points to a man. Women are more likely to use poison or arrange accidents. They don't like to get physically involved. These murders are a little too confrontational to fit the typical female profile.

"So here's my advice, Warren. Forget the serial killer profile. Look for a hit man, or a highly functioning charismatic sociopath. One theorist once described the kind of psychopath that you're seeking as the Machiavellian type: intelligent, manipulative, and narcissistic. Probably a man who is very sane—but angry—and who feels he's on a mission to destroy the evil church. Either that or he's somehow making money off these deaths."

"Thanks, Rose. That helps."

"Now pay the piper."

"Next session, I promise."

"Not good enough. I have an opening this Friday at seven P.M. I want you to sit right there and get that gorilla off your back. Deal?"

"Yeah, sure, deal." I was out of there. Maybe I'd come back.

I got home early enough to call Sally and fill her in on what Rose had told me. I didn't mention the price I was going to have to pay for that help. If I decided to pay it.

CHAPTER TEN

My phone welcomed me into Thursday. I was thrust out of a dream in which I was a steward on an airplane, and all the passengers were giant toads with Scottish accents. I'd need to be Jung to figure out what that meant.

The caller was English-speaking, too, but she sure was no toad. Sally said, "Rise and shine, Warren. I was up most of the night and I'm on my way over with lots of juicy tidbits on your case. So haul ass down to Brewed Awakenings and tell them to warm up my ham and cheese croissant. Order me a double mocha and I'll be there before your latte is brewed."

"Good morning, Sally. Thanks for rescuing me from the toads. I'll see you in ten minutes. Bye."

I could hear her ask, "Toads?" just before the headset hit the cradle.

Sally wheeled in on schedule and we took over the couch area in the back of the coffee shop. She was hauntingly beautiful. Those bags under her eyes gave her the Mimi-from-*La Boheme* look. But she was smiling. I still felt like crap.

"Warren, stop looking so grim. I come bearing tidings of great joy. We got one really good break. I have to boast a little. I'm so good at this game."

Her *joi de vivre* was resistable. "The caffeine and the grease are not yet starting to hit. I'm almost ready to process what you've got. Go ahead, Fill me in."

"Did you get a chance to meet with the Japanese girl?"

God, she knew how to hit a guy below the belt. I filled her in on my abortive interview. I also told her about my walk in the park with Edward.

That was enough talking for me. I said, "What did you find out that was so important that you had to stay up all night and then have the gall to disrupt my precious beauty sleep?"

She launched in. "In the packet you gave me there were five e-mails sent from the same location, a feed store in Kansas. Each e-mail was signed 'Barakiel.'

"Hackers know the guy who runs that feed store pretty well. He misconfigured his e-mail server, and his location has become famous as a blind lead, a dead end for you non-geeks. E-mail can originate from anywhere and appear to have been written at Walt Thomas's Feed and Tack.

"Luckily for you, my dear one, three years ago I created *Ghost Rider*. It's a benign virus program that hangs out in the server of a blind lead and analyzes incoming e-mails. I programmed this one to look for the tag line 'Barakiel.' By the way do you know who Barakiel is?"

"Not the serious cousin to that party-loving Bacchus, is he?"

"I doubt it. This is the angel who specializes in lightning strikes of retribution from God: Useful information for your next bible quiz. Where was I? Oh yeah, so once my program *Ghost Rider* finds its quarry, it follows that packet back to its true IP address. Then it comes to momma and tells me all about it. Oh, I can see it's still too early for you to follow this."

I guess she'd watched the incomprehension sweep across my face. "Why do all you techies love initials that no one else can understand?"

She sighed the weariness of the one-eyed Queen of the Blind. "Why didn't I fall in love with another hacker instead of a Luddite? Ah, well, I guess it's because we techies are all so boring. No one could accuse you of that."

"Yeah, you're so boring. Anyway, thanks, I think."

"Anyway, here's the translation: Ghostie tells me exactly where the computer is located, the location of the computer on which these e-mails were typed. With me?"

"I think I can barely keep up. English *is* my primary language."

"Hey, sarcasm. That's a sign that the old prefrontal lobe is warming up. Anyway, I got lucky. Three hours after I got *Ghost Rider* in place, Mr. Barakiel sent another missive. Here it is."

She handed me a copy of the e-mail:

```
To Satan's minions:
Father of Lies, you spread evil and dissent
across the land, and pollute the souls of
humanity. Today, you laugh at your sacrilege
and blasphemy. But soon the sword of the
righteous will sweep you from the face of
```

the earth, and you will burn in Hell among those you now worship.

—Angel Barakiel.

"Rather overwritten isn't it?"

Sally wasn't too concerned with my editorial opinion. "Right. But tracking this poetic message back home just led to another blind alley. The mail was coming from a public computer at the El Cerrito Public Library. This guy was pretty smart.

"So I hacked into the Contra Costa Library System database—what a sieve! But all libraries are. Someday I'll tell you about what happened when the Secret Service did a routine check on Jenna Bush and found out she was checking out books on bomb making. One of my finer moments!" Her face was shining.

"Hey, tell me about that!"

"Another time, maybe over a nice burgundy in front of my fire. Mmmm, sounds nice. Soon! Well, back to work. I looked for any patterns of checkouts at the El Cerrito branch a half hour before and after the five e-mails were sent. I got four possibles. A public records search eliminated all four: two were boys under twelve, one was a woman, and one was an eighty-six-year-old guy who had a disability license plate. Not that that detail would have stopped *me* from running somebody down, but I have a few years on him!

"Now Gramps or Billy could have been sending nasty e-mails. But probably neither one was driving cars over pedestrians, or pushing guys off cliffs. So it looked like our murderer wasn't in this crowd. Right?"

"Right."

"Wrong. Remember what Rose said: The killings didn't fit the pattern of a typical female serial killer. But what if this is the *GI Jane* of serial killers?

"So I went back to the woman who had made book transactions near the time of the e-mails. Pay dirt! She runs a gift store called Heavenly Deliveries specializing in all sorts of crap connected to angels. Her current name is Grace Westin. Blond hair, blue eyes, five-foot-seven, no glasses. Here's a copy of her driver's license picture."

I looked at the picture of an Aryan gal in her late twenties.

"Angels. Well, that explains Barakiel. Is she making any money at this?"

"Glad you asked! Her business is not profitable, but over the past five years she has unexplained bonus deposits every three months or so of three to six thousand dollars. She owns a dark green Lexus free and clear. Paid it off in six months. Rents a suite on Albany Hill looking out on San Francisco and pays eighteen hundred a month for the privilege of living there. Let's see, which of the two illicit professions might she be in, the oldest or the most ruthless?"

"You're like a Jack Russell terrier with this stuff, aren't you?"

"It's Parson's Russell terrier these days. Same dog, new name. Don't ask why. And, yes, I love the hunt. Her background check went no further than seven years. I don't know how this chick got the Westin ID manufactured but I had a hunch that she might have been stupid enough to keep her old date of birth: June 17, 1978.

"I did an outstanding-warrant check nationwide against that birthdate and found forty-seven rejects and one girl named

Gloria Wells from Helena, Montana. She had a very similar physical description, except that she was a brunette. She also had a juvie record as long as your arm, one that didn't get closed when she became an adult. That's pretty unusual. Adopted at birth, in and out of foster homes. Trouble from Jump Street. Her probation was revoked when she disappeared, and the felony warrant put out on her for armed robbery is still active ten years later. Interesting, isn't it? Here's her Web site and a map to her shop."

She handed me a Yahoo Mapquest map and a page bordered with cherubs and heavenly hosts titled "Heavenly Deliveries: The Closest Shop to Heaven!"

"Sally, you are amazing! And so damn cute at the same time!"

She beamed me one of those I-just-got-a-pony-for-Christmas smiles and said, "S'okay. I'd go crazy living in this chair if it wasn't for my work."

"Well, thanks for staying up all night to get this stuff."

"You don't understand, Warren. I live for this. When I'm out on the Net, I fly as free as anyone. The world spreads herself out before me. I soar through databases, mainframes, and global networks like an invisible albatross. It's magical, and I love it. So keep those cases coming, Philo Vance. I'll be here to back you up all the way."

We kissed farewell. Walking back to my pad I thought, *Hmm, if I didn't want to kill myself, this wouldn't be such a bad way to start the day.*

CHAPTER ELEVEN

I live in an eccentrically cute one-bedroom space on the third floor of an apartment building built right after the earthquake. (There was only one earthquake: 1906, the one that leveled San Francisco.)

My windows look out over the journalism building to the bell tower and the North Gate commons. It's a lovely view, if your deaf. Day or night, there is an ongoing symphony of buses shifting gears, car alarms mating, and gangs of students excitedly or drunkenly screaming at each other. Besides that, the only downside is the midnight fights that break out among wandering tribes of psychotic, homeless gypsies. I wouldn't live anywhere else!

But today it felt claustrophobic. I needed to walk. I needed to chew over everything Rose and Sally had handed me. And I needed a heavy dose of herbal antidepressant. Next Stop: Caffe Mediterraneum.

If you knew Berkeley, you might wonder why I would snub the perfectly adequate coffee shops near my apartment. For one thing they're too cheery. At the Med everyone is of one mind: "Give me caffeine in a dosage that would kill a small child." After ten minutes nursing my triple nonfat latte, I began to find meaning in my life. The coffee bean is God's antidote to suicidal ideation.

Two-thirds of the way through my second latte, and halfway through my copy of *The New York Times,* I was beginning to feel ready to carpe diem.

A woman's contralto voice interrupted my reverie. "Hello, Richard." I didn't need to look up. Thirty years hadn't erased those memories. Just hearing her made it hard to breathe: Veronique.

But of course I did look up. How could she be in her fifties? She was better looking than I'd remembered: close-cropped black hair, eyes that hovered between blue and green, marble-smooth skin, thick, perfectly shaped lips, and that same lush body I remembered much too well.

The past thirty years had aged her. But they had not robbed her. Sure, they'd etched lines a little deeper in her face. But they had not turned her into one of those dried apple dolls. Now she looked both experienced and passionate.

I tried to dissemble, "My name is Warren, you must have the wrong person."

She laughed. "I'm sorry . . . Mr. Ritter, isn't it? You must be right. This is just a case of mistaken identity. May I sit down?"

I just gestured to the empty chair. The two chairs at the front table of the Med looked like they were swiped from some baron's dining room—they were high-backed carved wood with rust-colored upholstery.

Veronique settled onto her throne and folded her legs. She

just sat there and watched me, a patient python. Finally I sighed and said, "You look unbelievably great, Veronique. Do you have a portrait of a wizened old crone in some attic somewhere?"

"No witchcraft, Richard—oops, I mean Warren. Sorry, it takes some getting used to, but I will try to remember."

"Thank you. Are you still Veronique?"

"Yes, I could never get into the alias trip. I fool around a little with my last name, but I like Veronique. It fits me too well to mess with."

This wasn't an accidental meeting. She was closing for the kill.

"So Q, what do you want?" I had lapsed into my old nickname for her without thinking.

"Ah, 'Q', I haven't heard that name in a few decades. Well, if you assume synchronicity isn't an explanation for our meeting like this you'd be correct. Yesterday I received this in the mail."

She handed me a piece of typing paper with a handwritten note on it:

Mistress of Satan:
God's wrath is focused on your sinful body.
Your skin shall crawl with maggots.
Your breasts shall sag and seep vinegar.
Prepare to die, harlot!
You will know my name is the Lord when I lay my vengeance upon thee.
(Ezekiel 25:17)

I still didn't want sole responsibility for this case. "Veronique, I'm not a cop. I told your brother that. I'm a fortune-teller, for Christ's sake. I know I said I'd help but really, I'm the wrong

61

guy for this job. You need a bodyguard. I know a great service in Oakland. They will give you twenty-four/seven protection. Valdez Security Systems, I have the number right here." I started to reach for my wallet.

She stopped my arm. I flinched a little at her touch. "Warren, we have already taken care of our protection. What we need from you, no, what *I* need from you is for you to track down the person who is committing these atrocities. Please, my life may depend on it."

Damn, I was so stuck in this mess. "How much do you know about these killings?"

"Not much. I was in Europe when they happened." She gestured toward the letter she'd handed me. "Its the next one I'm worried about."

This all sounded so melodramatic I should have cringed. But with her warm hand on my skin and her blue eyes looking deeply into mine, I was trapped, "Okay, was there any return address?"

"Yes, they put mine on it. But it was postmarked Oakland."

"I'll do some checking and get back to you. How can I reach you?"

"Why don't we have dinner together tonight, and you can tell me what you found out." I heard that annoying Barbra Streisand song in my head: *Well, a bit of dinner never hurt/But guess who is gonna be dessert.* I was afraid she was out for more than information. Still, she was my client.

I replied, "Sounds good. Where?"

"Why don't I have you to my place?"

I was pretty sure I wanted to stay as far away from her bedroom as I possibly could, for the sake of my current relationship.

"How about if I get us a window table at Skates for seven o'clock? It'll be under the name Ritter."

Was that a pout? "Okay, if that's what you want. How can I reach you if I need you?"

The idea of her needing me had a nice ring to it. And scared me. I gave her my cell phone number.

She ascended from her chair and glided out the door. I decided to go ahead and kill myself now, and avoid the tidal wave of shit heading toward me.

CHAPTER TWELVE

I chickened out. Instead of running down to BART and throwing myself on the electrified rail, I folded up the note she left me, stuck it in my backpack, and headed homeward across the campus.

I had to get to work on the Hightower case. The Hightower case? Who was I kidding? Now I was Sherlock Holmes or something. And where the hell was Watson when I needed him?

I got about ten feet from the cafe door when I heard a voice from across the street call out, "Yo, Warren, What's the hap's?" It was Leticia, my current nemesis. I waved and tried to walk on, but she cut across the traffic to talk with me.

"Hold up! Dude, I'm so sorry I busted your gig with the Priestess. I had no idea you were in the middle of a scam. I'm sorry."

"That's okay, Leticia. I had no business being there anyway. Why do you call her the Priestess?"

"Oh, it's an anime thing, you know, Japanese animation. It's my nickname for her. Miko means priestess in Japanese.

Warren, what are you doing messing with Miko? Are you crazy?"

"What do you mean?"

"Miko's connected. You know, like gangster, only in Japan they call it clan. She plays for keeps, and she's pissed!"

"Great. Okay, thanks. I'm pretty sure that I will do whatever is possible to avoid that girl, anyway. But I appreciate the warning."

"Hey, I gotta run. Just wanted to put a bug in your ear. Stay loose."

"You too, sweetie."

I was appreciating my network of friends, as I logged on to my e-mail. They were really going to miss me when I got plugged by some Japanese thug. Right under a very generous offer from the assistant prime minister of Nigeria was an e-mail from Sally:

```
Hey Nero: Hope you are hot on the trail. I
was so bushed this morning that I forgot to
remind you about my game tonight. Hey, bring
pom-poms. The Wheels of Fortune made it to
the semifinals. We have home-court advantage
and I need my favorite cheerleader to in-
spire me to a twenty-point game. Heather
will meet you out front with the tickets.
I'm going to crash or I'll be wiped for the
game. See you then, sweetie! Love, Archie
P. S. Ripley says bring her a dog bone.
```

I felt really guilty. For the past two hours no thought of Sally had entered my mind. I was much too obsessed with that ghost rider from my past. Although in my defense, she was a damn good-looking ghost. And now I was caught between a girl and a hard place. I had two dates for tonight.

An honorable and forthright man would call up, cancel the raven-haired ex-girlfriend and grab his pom-poms. I, on the other hand, whipped off an e-mail to Sally saying:

Oops! Sorry, honey. Bummer, I already set up a dinner meeting with my new satanic client. Have a great game, and call me when you get home, I want to find out about the forty points you scored single-handedly! Love you, Warren

All true, but I wasn't even trying to kid myself. My intentions were honorable, but I wanted dinner with Q. Such a mix of attraction, fear, obligation, and old memories. I knew I was making the wrong choice. So what.

I wondered where I would find a seamstress to embroider the red "A" on my shirt. I reread Sally's notes and then put them through my cross-cut shredder and flushed them down my toilet. Once I had made the mistake of leaving case notes pinned all over my apartment. They made great reading for the FBI when they broke in. These days I tried to keep everything in the collander I called my head. I logged on and checked out the Heavenly Deliveries Web site. Then I set off to snag me some angels.

El Cerrito stretches monotonously along San Pablo Avenue north of Berkeley. It's a necklace of mediocrity, strung with failed shopping centers, second-hand furniture shops, and Taco Bells, interspersed with an occasional shining jewel like Target or Home Depot. It has all the urban planning of a strip mine. But a strip mine trying to gentrify itself.

Boring suburban homes littered the hills, housing folks too poor to buy a house somewhere cool, like Berkeley, or too insipid to care where they lived, as long as the TV reception was good and they were close to shopping centers.

Heavenly Deliveries was located in one of those dying strip malls. To the left of it was a cell phone store whose windows were covered with garish posters in Spanish. To the right, a pet store, where you could watch anemic kittens lying lethargically in the corners of their dirty cages, victims of learned helplessness.

In stark contrast, the window of the angel store had a painted gold ribbon rippling all around the frame. The display consisted of cantilevered shelves filled with sculptures of angels singing psalms of joy, angles drying their wings, angels reading books, sleeping on clouds, playing musical instruments, basically doing everything but picking their noses and going to the bathroom. Overhead, several had taken flight and traveled in regular circles over the scene.

I liked watching the cats better.

When I walked in, I triggered the welcoming signal. No little bell hanging over the door. Instead the CD started spinning and some soprano launched into "Ave Maria." This was going to be a tough interview. I hoped I could make it through without gagging.

"Blessings and welcome to Heavenly Deliveries."

I was stunned. Her picture hadn't clued me in. This woman looked exactly like a slightly older version of my old girlfriend Cathy, the mother of my daughter. My heart slammed out a few staccato beats until my head told me that this couldn't be her.

The shop's proprietor was a blue-eyed blonde. She was a tall, big-boned, substantial woman. Her bright pink sweatshirt featuring a cherub waving from a fluffy cloud with her halo askew didn't slenderize the gal any. She wasn't obese, in that pasty, flabby way that is so common to this fast-food nation. She was solid. She looked like a countrywoman out of a Bruegel painting: powerful, buxom, and a little creepy. Not attractive, except that I felt drawn to her because of an old memory. Unlike Cathy, her energy and presence were commanding.

"Oh, hi, and blessings to you, too, I'm sure." I don't know how to respond to someone who greets me with "Blessings." This wasn't Thanksgiving.

"How can I help you find what you seek today?"

Social justice? Equal distribution of wealth and privilege? World peace? The end to hunger? Somehow I doubted that what I sought was going to be on sale today in this particular store.

"Well, actually I was looking for some tarot cards that might have angels on them. I hope you don't think that's witchcraft or something." I had already checked out her Web site. I knew she stocked them.

"Oh, no. I consult the cards regularly. It's a beautiful way to get in touch with the directions that our spirit guides give us?

We have two decks that contain a great deal of angel imagery. One is the Angelic Tarot. Printed on each card is a lesson in how to blend together the kabala, astrology, and inner wisdom. The other deck is more traditional, the Angels Tarot Deck, but the Major Arcana feature beautiful images of every angel mentioned in the bible. Then we also have Angel Power Cards, the Karma Angel Oracles, and the Angelic Voices Oracle Deck."

"That's quite a selection. Which deck do you prefer?"

"I love the imagery on the Angels Tarot Deck. Unfortunately we don't have one open right now."

I could play Mr. Sincere Seeker as well as anyone. "I'd really like to see the cards before I buy the whole deck. . . ."

She reached out and touched me, at the same spot Veronique had made contact earlier. I didn't flinch this time. "I'll tell you what I'll do. I think you will really like these cards. I can sense it. So I'll open this deck and if you don't want them I'll take them home and use them myself. How's that?"

"That's very kind of you. Thanks." She was setting me up; I was buttering her up. I knew I was walking out of there with a new deck of cards. Who cared, Edward was paying for them.

She drew out a wicked-looking dagger with curved edges and a cobra head on the hilt. I tensed. Did she know who I was? Was I about to be her next victim? She looked me in the eye, as if contemplating that action. Then she smiled and began to cut the wrapping on the cards.

I noticed her hands were red. "That's quite a sunburn you have there."

"I know, I'm such a ditz sometimes. I was south of the border earlier this week, and I kept forgetting to wear gloves when I was outside. Sunscreen just isn't enough for my skin. You're lucky you came in today. This is the first day this week I've been open."

"Were you down there for business or pleasure?" I was just fishing, not sure what I wanted to catch.

"That's not so easy to answer. I was down in Oaxaca contracting for some Black Madonna pottery statues, and some handmade rugs with images of angels woven into them. But you know, down there there's no separation between business and pleasure. I spent most of my time having a few lemonades and catching up with the latest news from the pueblo. The business was tacked on to the end, almost as an afterthought. It's a very loving place. Anyway, here are your cards. Aren't they beautiful?"

She spread them out on the counter in front of her. Some of them were striking. I would never use them on the street, but these were kick-ass angels. Michael was crushing the Devil's face in the dirt. "These are great. I'll buy them." I laid out the cash. "And since now I'm a patron of Heavenly Deliveries, you can call me Warren."

She slipped the currency into her pocket. Interesting bookkeeping system. "Hello, Warren. I'm Grace. So tell me, why do you like this deck?"

"The angels look like they're out of the Old Testament, powerful and dangerous." Then I thought I'd take a chance. I drew out the picture of an angel with a flaming sword about to whack apart a castle. It was Barakiel. "I like this card particularly. This is an angel to fear."

She looked at me for a long moment, sizing me up. I held her gaze, and tried not to think about that dagger in her hand. Then she made a tiny nod. I had just passed some test. She said, "Oh, if you like that one, I'll show you another deck. But this one is not for sale. It's been out of print for fifteen years or more, but an acquaintance of mine brought it to me from Germany."

She reached under the counter and brought out a dark red silk pouch. Opening it slowly, she reverently removed an oversized deck. She waited while I gathered my cards off the counter and then ceremoniously spread hers out.

I had never seen images like these. Each card was a work of art. Every icon emerged out of an empty background that was a blend of darkness and radiant gold. A black angel of death sat back on her heels, her face veiled, her elongated fingers enclosing a green radiant soul, about to be extinguished. An angel in a witch's hat held aloft a spear of light. Many of the faces looked determined and some were a little pissed. There was nothing saccharine about these twenty entities.

I pulled out the card marked Der Teufel. "Look, the Devil as a sensuous woman, flanked by naked male and female demons. I've never seen the feminine side of Satan before."

"I don't think the Lord of Lies is limited to only one gender. Do you believe in evil, Warren?"

God, here it was again. Is this the pop-up question of the week? This time I knew my audience and what she wanted to hear. "Yes. I hope I'm not going to offend you, you running an angel store and all. But I can't stand Pollyanna New Age do-gooders who go around spouting 'All is love' platitudes, and then go home and kick the dog or beat their kids. Evil exists all around us."

She nodded. "Don't worry about offending me. I eat my steak almost raw, and drink Wild Turkey straight up. And I know all about evil. That's another thing I loved about Mexico. The Mexican peasant in the streets knows the Devil exists. She has to battle with Satan and his minions daily. That's why I love these cards.

Look at these Warriors of the Light. These winged beings will stop at nothing to destroy that which is wicked. They inspire me."

She reached under the counter again. I watched carefully, still not sure of her intent. This time she pulled out a box and opened it. Inside were tiny chocolate angels playing an assortment of musical instruments.

She pushed the box toward me. "These are Belgian. Would you like some?"

I guess I'd passed the test. Unless she was trying to poison me. "No thanks, I'm on Atkins."

"Oh, I know, I need to do something like that. I have an incurable sweet tooth." She popped a viola-playing winged creature into her mouth.

I said, "These angels look like they really mean business. But it was easier in biblical times. The unholy were conveniently destroyed by angels and by the armies of the righteous. These days, it's harder to know who is working for Satan and who is just another lost, godless soul."

Her face began to redden and her eyes flashed. "Oh, they're not so hard to find. Minions of the Dark Lord flaunt their unholy doctrine. But you're right. God's not going to step down and smite them today. And no angels are going to show up with their flaming swords. No, these days God needs us to be his right hand!"

That was a pretty close to a near-confession. I didn't want her to get any more righteous, especially while she was still gripping that blade. Time for a change of topic. "Yes, it is the moment for the good to take a stand against evil, I agree. I have to get going soon, Grace, but I want to compliment you on your great Web site. You must be a real computer wizard."

She laughed. "Hardly. It's all I can do to write e-mail. The credit for that site goes to George. He's a twelve-year-old who I met one day. He was sitting beside me at the library computer lab. We've become good buddies. He taught me so much, and he did my whole site almost for free. I just had to buy him some programming software and a couple of gizmos for his laptop. He's a real hacker. Gosh, he knows so many tricks. Not all of them legal, mind you, but he means no harm. I don't know what I would have done without him!"

"He's a blessing, I'm sure. Thanks so much for all your help, Grace. And it's so great to find a person with such strong values. I admire you." *Lay it on, grab your cards, and get out of there before you start to giggle.*

"Thank you, too, Warren, and please come back again soon. It was very refreshing talking with you. Be blessed."

"Right." One short chorus of "Ave Maria" as I went out the door, and I was free. The more I'd talked with her the less I felt like I was with a Cathy clone, but still it was a weird experience. My past was bumping against me every day.

What were Rose's criteria? Intelligent, manipulative, and narcissistic. Maybe. On a mission to destroy the evil church. Again maybe. And little George was the computer geek who helped Grace disguise where she sent those e-mails from. This was fitting together quite nicely. Now Sally could check out Grace's trip to Mexico, and find out what she could about where she was during the times of the murders. I felt I was getting much closer.

As I drove home hurrying to get ready for tonight's date, I tried to keep my mind on the case. But I kept thinking of Veronique's wide eyes and long legs. Shame on me.

CHAPTER THIRTEEN

The city shimmered across the bay like the crown jewels. The Bay Bridge was a long string of diamonds stretching across the water toward our table. Skates was a trendy fish restaurant on its own pier in the Berkeley marina, overhanging the bay. Our table was next to the window. The only thing between us and San Francisco was a pane of glass and a hell of a lot of cold water.

Veronique looked even more dazzling in candlelight. She was in a cream linen shift that caressed her curves, with slits up the sides and a neckline that kept teasing me to imagine what lay just out of sight. Clothes that simple usually cost a mint. I was glad I'd dressed up for this meal.

She set down her Singapore Sling, moved aside my beer, and leaned across the table. The place was crowded and noisy; it made perfect sense that she needed to be closer to talk with me.

"Remember when we first met?"

I laughed. "I'm not likely to ever forget that night." The

mind is so inventive. I could almost imagine that, hidden in the fragrance of the perfume she was wearing, was the faintest whiff of tear gas. Oh, yes, I remembered.

I'd made that rapid transformation that happened to so many of us back in the sixties, from loyal American to angry activist. There's nothing like the threat of getting killed in a stupid, mindless war to wake one up. I showed up for the Chicago Democratic Convention of '68 ready to put my body on the line to wake up "Amerika."

By the fourth day of the convention, we'd learned how to handle the tear gas. We kept damp handkerchiefs in our pockets. When the fumes hit, we wore them like masks to breathe through. We knew to walk away from the cloud (running made you breathe too fast). We taught each other to keep our eyes open so that our tears would weep the chemicals from the surface of our eyes. I carried an oven mitt on a clip on my belt. I used it to grab the hot gas canisters that rolled toward me, and lob them back at the pigs.

For three days the cops had been bashing on us at Lincoln Park. They had smashed cameras and stopped television crews from entering, so the rest of the country didn't have a clue that their kids were being beaten and clubbed. But on Wednesday we got lucky. The cops went after us in front of the Hilton Hotel. One awesome television cameraman got away with a roll of fifteen minutes of violence. It made it right onto the networks.

Right after that massacre our cell started a march moving toward the convention center. The word was out and soon we were joined by more kids, a few McCarthy delegates, and about one hundred pissed-off Chicago bystanders. As long as we stayed on Michigan Street we had cameras on us, folks honking support, and soon we were a small army.

But once we got into the Loop it all started falling apart. The bystanders disappeared, the video crews were blocked out, and the cops came in, batons raised, and fired tear gas canisters right at us. The group started splitting up.

I got separated from my troops. The mob panic energy was rising. I could see that my pack of frightened demonstrators was getting herded into a trap. If I was going to escape, I needed to split off and go out on my own. I headed down an alley and almost made it to the end when three cops stepped in front of me and closed off my escape route. I spun around to backtrack and stepped right on top of a Coke bottle.

I hit the asphalt hard and tucked into a ball just before the clubs came down on me. Two gorillas hauled me up, and the third jabbed his baton into my diaphragm. While I was gasping for air, they dragged me out of the alley, cuffed me, and tossed me into a big truck filled with about twenty of my fellow demonstrators. I was off to jail.

"You okay? Have you caught your breath?"

I looked up into dark, blue-tourmaline eyes. She had pearl-colored skin and black hair down to her waist. I figured the cops had made a mistake. They'd tossed me into the van going to Heaven.

I said, "I can breathe, almost."

"Here, roll over. I'll get those things off you." I obeyed. There was a click and the bands of metal that were cutting off the circulation to my fingers suddenly dropped away.

I was impressed. "Hey, Houdini. How'd you do that?"

"Primitive locking mechanism. I could teach you that trick in half an hour." Her voice was low and urgent. And deliciously husky. "We don't have much time. We're getting out of here the next time that door opens. Some of these idiots huddled in the back over there are going to stay, but most of us are getting ready to rumble. Are you with us?"

My kind of people. "Let's rock and roll."

"Here's the gig. Since we all have been so well-mannered, the pigs have been getting lazy. For the fast three stops, two of them head for the front, while the third cop opens the door and stuffs in the next victim. So the minute that lock clicks, we throw ourselves against the doors. That should knock over Officer Porker. Then we just run like hell. Are you for it?"

"I'm outta here."

We didn't have long to wait. Good news, too. It sounded like there was a crowd outside. We could hear "Fuck the draft" and "Hell no, we won't go!" Our people were right outside. I wanted to be one of the guys who blasted open the doors, but I was too small. Instead, two halfbacks lined up and smacked the panels in perfect unison. The doors cracked open, bounced against the side of the truck, and flipped back to smash into our heroes as they were flying out of the van. Ouch! I was glad I missed that part of the adventure.

We poured out of there like paratroopers over Normandy. A dozen demonstrators in front of the paddy wagon had been taunting the other two cops. When they saw our escape they started cheering and surged toward the van. The two pigs dropped back to protect their partner, who was still rolling on the ground, squalling. We ran, and I stayed side by side with my Valkyrie princess.

Those same blue eyes were looking right into me now. She said, "Your face has changed: plastic surgery and age. You look even better than you did in the back of that wagon. Less militant, more vulnerable. It looks good on you."

"You're looking pretty damn good yourself. Now let's order dinner and I'll tell you all about my brilliant detection."

We both ate hickory-grilled wild sea bass with mango tapenade, resting on a thin bed of polenta and surrounded by roasted vegetables. I briefed her on Ms. Tashima and her Colt revolver, Heavenly Deliveries, and angelic Grace Westin, aka delinquent Gloria Wells. I downplayed the contributions of Sally and overdramatized my role as interrogator extraordinaire. I left out the humiliating experience in Miko's living room. Truth belongs to whoever writes the history.

Veronique was suitably impressed. She closed her eyes as she savored her last spoonful of soft, warm chocolate cake with vanilla bean gelato. Then she opened those brilliant blue pools. I began to notice how wide the pupils of her eyes were getting. This was not a drug reaction. She was thinking about something more hormonal than detection.

Ten years ago I would have hopped into bed with her. Hell, maybe ten months ago. Before Sally. I knew I'd already crossed the line by lying to her about this date. Still, I felt that I could manage my way out of that. But if I slept with Q, all trust would go flying out the window. Sometimes the big head above the neck can overrule the little head below the waist.

"Well, that's all I have to report for now. Can I walk you to your car?"

She got up with that cobra movement and took my hand. Electrons jumped the gap. I was pretty sure my resolve would hold out.

The hot wind off the bay didn't help settle things down. I was wishing she'd let go of my hand. I kept getting these orgone discharges up my arm.

She had parked toward the back of the lot. It felt like we were walking for days into the shadows. We could hear the clatter of rigging from the sailboats in the marina. Suddenly, a dark car, parked right in front of us, pinned us with bright halogen headlights. Then the motor went on and the car started rolling past. I just had time to notice that the driver's window was all the way down when I saw a flash and heard the crack. Then Veronique screamed and went down at my feet.

CHAPTER FOURTEEN

Shit!" she yelled.

"Veronique, are you hit?" I dropped to the pavement, reaching around for her.

"I tripped. I think I sprained my goddamn ankle. What was that noise?" I looked up, just in time to catch a glimpse of the car as it passed under a streetlight. Dark four-door sedan. It could have been a Lexus. Definitely not a Z-3. The light that was supposed to illuminate the license plate was off.

"We were just shot at. I mean you were just shot at. Thank God this time he missed. We've got to call the cops."

Veronique said, "No cops! Neither one of us wants cops investigating us. Shit, this ankle hurts. And my nylons are ruined."

She talked me out of police involvement very easily. Besides, what was there to investigate? The car was gone. The slug was in the bay somewhere. As I was helping her to her feet, I noticed a round stick on the ground underneath her. That must have been what she tripped on. It probably saved her life. She had a decent cut on her knee which was already swelling. I took off my tie and wrapped it around her leg. Silk, but who cares?

"Warren, I can't drive. Fuck, that hurts! Look, leave me here and go get your car. I promise I won't get shot at again. I need you to drive me home tonight. Tomorrow, my brother, or somebody from the church will get my car. Here, I'll lean against this tree. I'm fine. Now go, and hurry, please!"

I ran across the lot, keeping an eye out for any sedans sneaking their way back. I left a patch of rubber as I peeled out of my space, in a hurry to get back to Veronique. As I helped her into the passenger seat she winced. "Not a very romantic way to end an evening. I'm a clumsy idiot, even if I'm a very lucky idiot."

We didn't say much on the drive to her place, a little house set in the backyard of a Berkeley craftsman. In the early sixties, the building codes were lax and many of these "in-law" rental units got slapped together to help pay the mortgage. This one was nicer than most.

She leaned on my arm as we made our way past the main house to a two-story dollhouse. The bottom room was a kitchen/dining/living room with a Danish modern freestanding fireplace in one corner. The walls were mostly panes of glass. It was too dark to see what they looked out on. A wooden spiral staircase rose to what was probably her bedroom. I was ambivalent about confirming this assumption.

"You're the knight-errant. Sit there and I will bring you a chalice." She pushed me toward the long tan leather couch positioned in front of the fireplace. I sat down, and then I noticed that the house was chilly. There was no other heater in the room, so I asked, "Mind if I make a fire?"

Somehow in spite of her injury she had managed to make it

up those stairs. Her voice came from above me. "I'd love it. Kindling is in the covered tin can next to the fireplace and there's more wood in the big box to the left of the coffee table. I'll be right down."

I heard her come down the stairs as I began assembling the teepee of kindling for the fire. Then, I heard pots clanking and water boiling, but I was absorbed in getting a fire going in this cranky, not-so-modern fireplace. Finally I got a good draft, and the wood caught.

The next thing I knew she had coiled onto her side of the couch. She had slipped into something that shimmered in silver and aquamarine. It might have made her more comfortable, but it was playing hell with my comfort level. All I could do was wonder if it was the only article of clothing she was wearing. She held a steaming drink toward me. "The fire looks great, Richard. Now come join me. Remember this drink?"

Call me picky, but I couldn't afford people using my old name. "It's Warren, Veronique, please."

I sat next to her, with an appropriate gap of air between our bodies, and took the mug. The scent of French roast, Kahlua, tequila, and a hint of cinnamon hit me hard. It took me right back to a time before my life went all to hell. One delicious weekend back in 1969 Veronique and I slipped away from the Weather Underground commune. I rented a rundown cabin right on the beach on the tip of Cape Cod for the weekend. It rained the whole time we were there, which was perfect. We spent many hours experimenting to perfect the ultimate Mexican coffee.

"This is the best medicine for broken knees ever invented. Taste it, Warren, it's even better than the ones we created. We used Gold and *Commemerativo*. Well, Cuervo *'La Reserva'* is ten times smoother."

I squirmed as I remembered what else we experimented with that weekend. Drinking any alcohol was going to turn this evening into a highly combustible event. I knew my bipolar cycles well enough to know that I was riding a manic surge. If I added alcohol to the excess of norepinephrine already flooding my poor brain, I was going to end up with short-term ecstasy and long-term regret.

I tried cooling her jets. "Veronique, I don't get it. You were just shot at. You could have been killed. And now you're doing sultry. Didn't almost getting murdered affect you at all?"

She placed the drinks on the small table in front of us. Her face was blank for a moment. "I'm trying not to think about it." Then she looked at me, and tears started forming. "I really don't want to think about it. It's too scary."

She started to cry, and I held out my arms. She wrapped herself around me, and sobbed on my shoulder. I could feel the dampness as the tears soaked through my shirt. Her body trembled in small sobs and she clung tighter. What I couldn't feel was any sign of a bra under that thin silk. Damn.

Most women look like shit after they've cried. Their faces get all blotchy from grimacing. Their mascara makes railroad tracks down their cheeks. This was the first time outside of the movies that I saw a woman look more radiant and glowing after a good sob session. Waterproof mascara for sure.

She took a tissue from the table and made what little repairs were necessary. Then she said, "I don't often let myself fall apart like that. I guess I really trust you, Richard, or Warren or whatever you like to be called. Thanks for just holding me."

"Hey, no problem. Well, I should be going now."

"Wait, don't run off. I don't think I'm quite ready to be alone. Just have one drink with me."

I lifted the mug to my lips and faked drinking a sip. "Mmm, you're right, even better than I remember."

She slithered over so that she was tucked next to me, and we were both facing the fireplace "Nice fire, Warren. You were always good at that."

I felt her hand rest itself on my leg. Okay, time to fish or cut bait. Or, as Tex, my captain on a fishing boat in Alaska liked to say, "It's nut-cutting time."

I rose, bent over, and gave her a comradely peck on the forehead. I moved back as she arched up to kiss my lips, and said, "I'm bushed, Q. I've got to get home. I'll call you or your brother to check in as soon as I hear anything. Good night and take care of yourself. I know this has been a real shock for you."

I was near the door, backing away as I talked. She just watched me, her expression inscrutable. She said nothing as I let myself out.

CHAPTER FIFTEEN

I couldn't go home. I'd just lie there twisting in my sheets all night. So I parked up near the seminary and headed for the university. Walking the roads through the campus at night was like a Sierra Club hike through Dante's *Inferno*. Tall eucalyptus trees arched over the trail as it plunged down to flowing streams or rose to wander across misty lawns. Vents in the middle of the road discharge hot gases creating moist walls of steam you must break through as you walk deeper into the campus. The only sounds are the pulse of an occasional sprinkler, and the incessant low rumble of restless traffic traveling far-off highways.

I had the place to myself. There were no gaggles of giggling sophomores or packs of drunken bicyclists to contend with. I could stretch out and stride into the darkness, walking off the tension of being the target for attempted murder and attempted seduction.

I thought about the differences between men and women. Women will never understand men. They just can't get over the first hurdle. I think it is a difference in wiring installed in our genes over tens of thousands of years on the African savanna.

Women know, as an irrefutable fact, that the whole of creation is held together by webs of relationships. Dogs and children curl up next to us for something more than reasons of survival. We are born, live, and die, connected to each other and to all living and nonliving beings.

Guys don't know that, except for maybe one or two mystics. Sure they give it lip service. Romantic poets and modern New Age guru-marketers write inspiring books all about love, ecology, and interdependence. But they don't know it, not as irrefutable fact in every cell of their bodies.

Men know something else. You must accomplish your goal. It doesn't matter if your goal is running an antelope off a cliff, lobbing a grenade into a machine-gun nest, or coming in under projected expenses in this month's financial review. You are only as good as your accomplishments. How you feel, what you've learned, how you've grown, or how much other people love you: All that crap is irrelevant. What have you done today? That's what matters.

Women (and I'm just referring here to the ones who aren't trying to pass as men) think that this attitude is unforgiving, workaholic, perfectionist, arrogant, and ultimately very selfish. For the sake of the goal, men continually sacrifice their kids, their friends, their mates, and anyone else who tries to get too intimate with them. Men are willing to shatter relationships if that's what is necessary to get the job done. That really pisses women off.

Which brought me, in my pop-psych reflections, to the topic of Veronique and my girlfriend, Sally. Seduction, for a woman, is about creating a relationship. Seduction for a man is about achieving a goal. Now Veronique was one juicy goal. I had no doubt that attaining it would be memorable. And tragic.

And Sally would find out about it, I had no doubt. Then she would have her dog tear my throat out. No, that's not true. She would just leave me forever. Not a lot of gray area with that girl. I had pushed her limits once, and I knew I wasn't going to get a second chance. She had too much at stake. And now I'd already lied to her. A sin of omission is still a sin. I might be a lame-duck boyfriend and not even know it.

Why was I with her anyway? My main life goal for thirty years had been to stay under the radar of the authorities. Last spring, I had the FBI investigating me, my name was in the papers, and for a couple of days there was a statewide manhunt on for me. I should have burned all ID linking me to Warrren Ritter and disappeared.

Instead, I stayed on in Berkeley. Why? Because I wanted to get to know Sally better. What a lame excuse. And we still hadn't crossed home plate yet.

I didn't have a goal with Sally. That felt weird. Lately my life was more about finding things out about myself than about achieving some goal. I was tired of running. I cared about Heather. I'd discovered that I was happiest just hanging out at Sally's place. At least I hadn't gone out tonight and made a complete ass of myself.

I got home, a little less wired. As I walked in, I heard the beep of my cell phone on the small table in the entryway. I had two messages on voicemail.

Who wanted me? Sally, wondering where I was? Veronique, giving it one last shot? The president, calling to ask me for a reading? I hit the button.

One for three. The first message was Sally. "Warren, glad you didn't come. We sucked, and I blew it for my teammates. I don't want to talk about it, so don't call. We'll talk tomorrow. Right now I'm very, very grumpy. Better yet, come over for lunch. I may feel halfway human by then." Whew, I was off the hook for bailing on her. I felt more than a twinge of guilt.

Then came message number two. "Richard, this is your sister. I have something to say to you. Call me."

Who died? Tara had that kind of tone in her voice. Among all the other things that happened last spring, my sister had shown up on the scene, madder than hell. She had to be restrained from broadcasting my true identity to the world. She sprang another big surprise on me: I was a father, and I was about to become a granddaddy. Then she clammed up, furious at me for disappearing for thirty years. I hadn't heard from her in months. My sister was about as warm as a great white shark. Wait a minute. I may be maligning the shark family with that comment. Let's say she has a bit of an anger-management problem.

I'd figured out who my daughter's mom was. Then I had a private investigator find out where my daughter and her husband were living, and what the due date of the kid was. Then I backed off, and waited for my sister to make the next move.

I'd sent her a couple of letters since then, but she only responded once. Back in June she called my number and told me that I had a grandson and I better stay the fuck away from that family. Now she was back.

"Hi, sis."

"Oh, it's 'shyou. You're calling pretty damn late."

She sounded drunk. I don't think I had ever heard my sister drunk. There was hope for her yet. "Sorry, sis. I was busy getting shot at and didn't get back home until now. How are you?"

"Shot at? Good. I mean I'm good, not you getting shot at is good. Well, actually not good. Damn, I wish you'd called a bottle ago."

"Wine, I hope."

"Chardonnay. Anyway why did I call? Oh yeah. Mom died. Alzheimer's finally finished the job. I didn't wanna invite you to the funeral. You didn't earn the right to attend. Besides, it might 'blow your cover,' right?"

I said nothing. This call really sucked.

"But that's not why I called. I decided you should meet your daughter and grandson. No. that's not quite right. I decided you should call your ex-girlfriend and tell her you're alive, and let her decide whether or not you should meet Fran and Justin. And Orrin, too. That should be very funny. Anyway, I'm tired of playing God over this. You probably already know this, but Fran's mom is Cathy Witkowski. She took back her name after the divorce. Here's her number . . . Where the fuck? . . . It's around here somewhere. Shit. Oh, here it is."

I jotted it down while she slowly enunciated the numbers.

"Call me in about a month. Or not. Bye." Click.

Great timing. I'd had enough for one day. I didn't want to deal with this additional mess. I stripped, fell into bed, pulled the pillow over my head, and crashed.

CHAPTER SIXTEEN

She was much too wired to sleep very long. Before dawn she headed into Emeryville, to her roost at the counter at Denny's. She ordered coffee and a Belgian waffle with strawberries and whipped cream.

Tomorrow was the big day. A couple of evenings ago she had "accidentally" run into her next victim at a reading at Mama Bear's, the local lesbian bookstore and hangout. The poor girl was plain, lonely, and only too eager to invite a guest to her Santa Cruz mountain cabin for the weekend.

As she savored the tartness of the red berries she smiled. She liked playing God, or at least playing Kali. She'd lightly roasted and salted the poisonous nuts from Mexico. She would improvise the arson after she got there.

After she finished her breakfast, she ordered another coffee and looked around the restaurant. There was a table of black men in suits bullshitting each other, three white guys in some kind of dark green industrial uniforms grimly drinking their coffee, the same old geezer she had seen a couple of days ago (did he live here?), and a dad with his two daughters: one a preteen with violet hair, trying to look superior to this riffraff, and the other, a blonde little tyke incessantly asking her father questions. He must have the kids this week, and he's too lazy to cook breakfast. She pulled out her journal and began to write.

Anthony Mulhaven, Mexico City's sleaziest expat, came through for me just like I knew he would. I have enough of these "psychic nuts" to knock off everyone in this restaurant. Hey, old man, you want something to chew on? I know if I offered it to him, he would take it. People are brainless.

Most people are stupid sheep, just bleating and yearning to be led around. They are lost without a guard dog to tell them what to do. The sheep are so many, and the Border collies are far too few.

And the she-wolf, up on the bluff, watching the flock, waiting for a good plump candidate for dinner; she is the rarest of all.

The rules are different for the sheep, for the dogs, and for the wolf. Sheep have to get along. So they all love one another, share each other's grass, and teach their lambs to respect their good friends the dogs. They have to obey, and they obey all the way to the slaughterhouse.

The collies are in a more difficult position. They have the choice to use their fangs for good or for evil. But it's not real choice. Take one bite of mutton and the shepherd will shoot you where you stand. Guard dogs have to be strong, but they also have to be good.

The wolf obeys no one but herself. Screw the divine shepherd in the sky. Laugh at the herd mentality. Ignore the morality of the righteous. Just take what you need.

94

I'm another species: homo lupis. I am the forerunner of the next stage in human evolution, no longer a slave to my body, my mind, or my heart. I see the hypocrisy of ethics, the illusion of goodness, and the primacy of power and control.

I am an expert in manipulating the less-evolved members of my genus, the slaves: homo servilus; and the controllers: homo perfectus. I could lead them, inspire them, enrage them, or magnetize them based on my plans and my desires. But I do not care about them. And I owe loyalty to no one.

She closed her book, and looked back at the one-parent family finishing their breakfast. The older girl met her eyes and then quickly looked away. Lupis thought to herself, *I was fucking my father when I was her age. The big taboo, even in our society. It kept him in very tight control. And control is all that matters.* Leaving a small tip, she walked out of the restaurant and into the dawn-stained morning.

CHAPTER SEVENTEEN

Four horrible dreams. In one dream Sally pulled out a tiny derringer and shot me. In the next I was out at the end of the rifle range where I first learned to shoot. I was changing targets, when I heard the range master say, "Commence firing. Fire at will." I screamed and ducked as bullets flew over my head.

Then came the old reliable nightmare that haunted me all year. One man stumbling toward me, with blood pulsing from a bullet wound in his neck. The other man crawling over a wall to trap me, his neck torqued at a crazy angle. I can't move.

I don't remember too much about the last dream except the ending. I got a call on my cell phone. Sally was telling me that she could walk again, and didn't need her chair anymore. I was running over to her house through the rain to celebrate. I saw a crumpled heap on the sidewalk. As I got closer I saw who it was. The dream ended with me kneeling on wet pavement, sobbing. Sally lay dead in front of me.

I woke up at 5 A.M., feeling like roadkill. A two-hundred-pound anchor of heavy sadness lay upon my chest. At the foot of the bed I imagined that I could see the psychological three-man firing squad hired by my inner hanging judge, all dressed in the uniforms of the French Foreign Legion, raised their rifles.

One by one they opened fire: "Warren, you're a complete idiot. Who made you some character out of a John MacDonald novel, punching out the bad guys and stoically saving the fair maiden? You're a short, scrawny loser who has made nothing of his life. Just ask Miko."

The second one shot out with, "Look at you lying there, you pathetic wimp. Your only claim to fame is that you have kept running from the cops for thirty years. Hey, dickwad, nobody cares but you. Everybody has forgotten you. The Weather Underground was sophomoric, with their ridiculous little plans to save the world, support the Black revolution, and overthrow imperialism. All your fellow revolutionaries are managers at McDonald's and damn glad to have any job. The pigs won, and you're nothing but an outdated joke."

The third finished me off with, "You never did have the guts to grow up. Instead you spun out some dramatic, paranoid scenario about your romantic life as a fugitive. You don't have the guts or the maturity to settle down, get married, raise a family, and make a productive citizen out of yourself. Instead you hold all those virtues in contempt and glorify irresponsibility, delinquency, and immature lawlessness. You're pathetic."

With dread, I recognized what had happened inside. It had been building since yesterday. My depression was in full force. Most of the time I'd rather be manic-depressive than normal. The life of a "normal" non-bipolar person is dreary and pointless as far as I am concerned. Maybe once or twice in their lives they will really wake up and see the radiant majesty of this precious world in which they live. The rest of their lives are just bad television.

I live inside fireworks. But there's a hell of a price for the bursts of intense aliveness that make the tapestry of my life so colorful. On mornings like this one, the bill comes due. After visiting the peaks, the crash downward is even more excruciating. I'd been on a gentle upward slope for about a month. Now I was falling down the dark cliff on the other side.

I'm what they call a rapid-cycler manic-depressive. That meant my moods last weeks rather than months or years. That's the good news and the bad news. When the dark angels come to visit, life is almost unbearable. The self-hatred is brutal. The three executioners at the foot of my bed were going to greet me every morning until the antidepressants kicked in.

And that would take at least two weeks. I didn't dare rush things. I knew what happened if I started giving myself a full-strength dose of Paxil: I could bring on a manic spike taller than the Eiffel Tower. I would feel great for a couple of days and then really plunge, down below where the antidepressants could reach me.

If I went the other way, overdosing on mood stabilizers, that could make the depression worse. Again, I risked sinking into the territory of abject misery, where the suicide sirens tried to lure me into the .45-caliber instant solution to all unhappiness. Whatever I did, I needed to do it gradually. That meant toughing out a sad, dank month ahead.

I dismissed the firing squad, pried the anchor off my heart, and rolled out of bed. Early this year, when I caught the last murderers, I was riding a manic rocket. Nothing could stop me. Today, this murderer could probably walk up to me and confess, and I'd probably just shrug and go back to bed.

It was Friday. Usually that means no chores. But I had blown off laundry day yesterday. At least I could go through the motions of pretending that life mattered. I kissed off stretching and meditation. Who cared; I was going to die soon anyway and the journey toward enlightenment was nothing but a marketing scam perpetrated by LA-based publishing houses.

When I got down into the basement with my load, it seemed like too much work to walk back up three flights of stairs to my place. It was hours before the coffee shops opened. In a futile attempt to be useful, I began to clean out the apartment building's communal laundry room. Doggedly, I threw away all the empty boxes of soap, discarded several unmatched sox, and two pairs of dusty shorts. I carefully disposed of a moldy, infected dish towel and I tossed out a rusty bicycle pump. Then I scrubbed down the greasy linoleum.

Underneath the sorting table, on my hands and knees, I discovered a boarded-over hatch door in the wall, just a couple of feet tall. Being momentarily curious, I pried off the flimsy wooden bar that had been held on by two rusty nails. It served as a completely inadequate barrier. Feeling a bit like Alice after she ate the cake with currants, I opened the small door.

The rusted hinges shrieked alarm at my intrusion, but I got the hatchway open, and crawled into a cement-walled room. I could barely see. Beams of light shafted down from above. I could make out a larger door across the room.

Soot covered the floor. The only light was sun streaming through the slats of two cellar doors. I held one hand up to a wedge of this sunlight and saw that fine black dust covered my skin.

I was in an unused coal bin. I bet the other door opened up to the furnace room, but when I tried, it was locked from the outside. These days the furnace ran on gas, and this room was unused and forgotten. Rather anticlimactic. I would have loved to discover an old footlocker crammed full of *The Strand* magazines from the 1890s. Too fertile an imagination. Well, enough archeology.

I crawled back into the laundry room and jammed the small, crudely-built door closed. I was a mess. I walked upstairs, after carefully cleaning my sneakers so that I didn't leave a trail of black footsteps.

I dumped my filthy clothes in the bin and took a long shower. What a stupid messy adventure. Right now I had a need for speed. I wasn't up to the brisk jog across the campus. I stumbled back down the street to Brewed Awakenings, ordered a triple-shot mocha and a couple of ham-and-cheese croissants, and headed for the couches. In a couple of weeks these jeans were going to be a lot tighter.

Fortified by butter, chocolate, and caffeine, I figured it would be the perfect time to give the mother of my daughter a little surprise. I kind of hoped she would hang up on me. Misery loves more misery.

I trudged down to the pay phone on the corner. I should have been more cautious and gone across town, but I didn't really care. Let them jail me. I sighed and dialed the number my sister had given me.

"Good afternoon, Witkowski residence."

Oh, my God, it was her. She sounded untouched by the decades, as cheery as ever.

"Ah, Cathy Witkowski?"

"Yes?"

"Look, Cathy, I'm really sorry about calling you out of the blue like this after thirty years, but this is Richard."

"Richard? Who? Richard Green! Oh my God, it is you. I recognize your voice. But you died in that bomb explosion."

"Evidently not."

"What was it, some kind of amnesia?"

What a convenient excuse. I wish I'd thought of that. I could say "Yes!" but eventually my sister would find out and I would be back in the doghouse. Nope, no shortcuts. Only the truth will do. Or at least a part of the truth.

"No, Cathy, nothing so noble. When that apartment building blew up, I ran away. I used it as a way to disappear from a situation that I couldn't handle. I've been on the run since then. I'm sorry. I tricked you and everybody."

There was a long sigh. Then she said, "Oh, Richard. There's a lot you don't know."

"Actually I *do* know. My sister found me early this year. She told me about my daughter and about my grandson. But she made me swear not to contact them until she'd decided what to do. Last night she gave me your number. I guess I'm calling to say I'm really sorry for disappearing and leaving you with a baby to raise. I never would have stayed away if I'd known that she existed."

I hoped fervently that that was true.

Cathy said, "I didn't want you to know. I don't know how many nights I've laid awake replaying the last time you were in

102

town. I was so scared to tell you. When you died, I was a little relieved. At least, I wouldn't have to feel guilty about keeping this secret from you. And I also felt horrible. You died never knowing you were a father. God, you're alive. This is so strange. Did you . . ."

A large delivery truck geared up the hill, drowning out whatever else she was saying. I was grateful for the interruption. I didn't want to answer any of her questions. Not in the mood I was in. Once the truck was far enough up the street that I could hear her voice, I said, "Sorry, I didn't hear that last part. Look, Cathy, I know this is really a shock. How about if I let you digest this a little and call you back tomorrow? Would that work for you?"

"Oh, Richard. I mean—a part of me doesn't want you to hang up. I'm afraid that you will disappear again. But, yes, okay, I *am* overwhelmed. I don't know what to say."

"Cathy, I won't disappear. I have a favor to ask. I have gotten myself into a jam in my life. I really need for you not to tell other people that I'm still alive. I can't explain right now, but it could be dangerous for me if some people found out that I was still alive."

"Richard, of course. If that's what you need my lips are sealed. The last thing I want is anything bad to happen to you."

"Thanks, Cathy. I can't tell you how important it is that you keep all this confidential."

I didn't feel like being nice to anybody, but she was really showing up like a trooper, so I added, "And thanks for not ripping into me. I really appreciate how great you're taking all this."

She said, "Oh, Richard, I'm just glad to hear your voice!"

She's so nice. "How about I call you around seven tomorrow evening, that's ten your time, I think. Is that too late?"

"No, Richard, that will be fine."

"I promise. No more disappearing acts. Scouts' honor."

"Do you cross your heart with buttercups?"

"I cross my heart with Butterfingers."

It was a phrase from our pillow talk when we were lovers. God, why do we always remember the most embarrassing sentimental crap?

"Okay, tomorrow then. Good-bye, Richard."

"Good-bye Cathy."

CHAPTER EIGHTEEN

y cell phone was beeping to welcome me back into my apartment. The message was from Mr. Hightower himself.

"Good morning, Warren. I hope you survived dinner and attempted murder with my sister last night. Now you know firsthand how imperative it is that we expose this maniac as soon as possible. I realize that this is all terribly unfair to you, but we're desperate.

"However, our plight isn't the only reason I'm calling today. Remember in the park when you displayed your abysmal ignorance about my religion? It would please me greatly if you could attend two events which may lead to a better understanding of our philosophy.

"The first is a public forum we are holding to inform select members of the general public about our church. It might help dispel some of your misconceptions about the Church of Satan, and our particular denomination, the Fellowship of the Arising Night. We are meeting at noon this Saturday at the church.

"The second is a private ritual we are conducting to help you in your quest to bring the killer to justice. I can promise you no goats will be slaughtered or innocent children despoiled. That will happen Sunday evening. I sincerely hope you can make it to both events." He then gave me an address on Sacramento Street in Berkeley.

Well, it beat spending Saturday in bed, which was the probable plan for tomorrow, assuming that my melancholy stayed as thick as it was right now. I wrote the address on a Post-it and stuck it on my door. That way I might see it in the morning at the beginning of my quest for caffeine.

I checked my watch. I was going to have to hurry if I was going to get to Sally's by noon. I hated to hurry in this mood. Hurrying seemed hardly worth it. I was dreading this visit anyway.

So I was late. Ripley gave me a good licking at the front door after Sally buzzed me in. Sally was next, with a delicious kiss well worth bending over for. Then she pulled back and looked at me. "There's something wrong. What is it?"

I had a list, and I didn't want to start with the one that was going to piss her off, so I said, "A few things, but mostly my depression came back. Sorry."

"Hey, sweetie, it's not your fault. I know this is part of the territory. Come on in and sit, I've got lunch almost ready."

I handed her the *Mistress of Satan* handwritten letter that Veronique had received before she could wheel away. "Wait, look at this. Is there any way you can trace the sender? No return address, but I think it was postmarked in Oakland."

Sally beamed. Some folks get excited seeing a Picasso or a cherry pie. My girl loved any problem that required an extensive, complex, computer program to solve. She pulled a keyboard out of the back pocket of her chair. She typed away furiously as she talked to me.

"This is great. I get to give John Hancock a trial spin. It's my new graphology recognition program. A couple months ago I started a project to see if I could link a handwriting analyzer program with the signatures on file in the California Driver's License database. I was going to use it to search for a missing girl, but the guy who was paying me found his daughter through an ad in the *LA Times,* so I never got a chance to try it out. This will be a great first test. Okay, it's launched. This is going to be fun. Thanks. No charge for this one."

She tucked her wireless keyboard back into its compartment and wheeled over to her flatbed scanner. She positioned the letter, hit a few keys, and then headed toward the kitchen. "We've probably got an hour or so before we can expect any results. Have a seat in the dining room and I'll be right out."

She brought in a salad of chunks of chicken, currants, pecans, avocados, and golden raisins over a bed of arugula and spinach. The curry vinaigrette was perfect with it. Last week I would have been raving. Today it tasted like tart cardboard.

We chatted, or rather Sally chatted and I tried to arrange my face in appropriate receptive expressions. She talked about her missed shots in last night's game; about Heather's new high school teachers; about a training in cancer detection through scent that she was putting Ripley through; and about her latest attempt to divert funds from the Elliot Institute, an anti-abortion organization dedicated to spreading horror stories about post-abortion trauma, and deposit them to the International Planned Parenthood Federation. She had siphoned $6,000 out so far without anyone noticing it. These are the kinds of fun, recreational activities that give her life meaning.

Then we got down to business. Sally said, "I've got another chunk of data about our Japanese friend. Miko grew up in California. When she was fifteen she moved back to Japan. She has some very interesting family ties. She's a cousin of Takado Tashima, Saiko-Komon to one of the most powerful clans of the Yakusa in Japan. That translates as chief administrator for the Japanese mob. She probably knows how to use that .357 pretty well. Don't piss her off!"

Too late. "I already know that. Don't worry, Sally, I'll be careful."

"Good. With her connections she could arrange a contract on you in about five minutes."

Great.

Sally's computer gave a chime like Big Ben. She smiled. "Hey, we got at least one hit." She wheeled over and handed me a sheet containing three possible matches, complete with addresses, phone numbers, birth dates, and a picture from their driver's licenses. Lauren Maram lived in LA, was twenty-one, and looked very goth. She was probably pro-Satan. Cross her off the list for now, unless she recently became born-again. Rev. Sharon Morrison, a mousy, thirty-seven-year-old woman in glasses, lived in Hayward; a possible candidate, Henry Daggert, forty-two, lived in Gualala, wherever the hell that was, and had red hair and a crooked smile. Who knew about that one?

"Thanks, Sally, you're a genius!"

"Hey, no problem. When did you get this letter?"

Oh, oh. Here it comes. Bombs away. "Veronique tracked me down at Caffe Med and gave it to me."

Sally wasn't smiling. "Oh, and when did this happen?"

Well I might as well dump the whole pile all at once. "Yesterday morning. And I had dinner with her last night, to report about my visit with the angel lady. Someone shot at us in the parking lot. And no, I didn't sleep with her, if that's what you're wondering."

Sally was unsmiling. "You didn't tell me she was back in the picture. I guess she didn't like girls all *that* much. And you said on the phone that you were having dinner with your client, carefully omitting the gender of said client. Warren, what the hell kind of bullshit is this?"

I didn't even have the energy to be defensive. "I'm sorry, Sally. I should have told you right off. Not that there's anything going on. But I wasn't clean about it. I do apologize."

Sally looked at Ripley. "*Staan!*" This was not good. She had just pulled out her canine armament and pointed the barrel right at me. Ripley leaped up and ran over to her master. Then she stood next to Sally's chair, alert, with her leg muscles quivering. At Sally's next command she would launch herself at anything or anyone. Since I was the only one there her choice of targets was limited.

Then Sally looked back at me. "Fuck you, Warren. You're just like all the rest of them. I have zero tolerance for liars. Now listen carefully, Mr. Ritter. Say one more word and Ripley will be all over you. And there will be blood on the floor. Goddamn you!

"I'm going to tell you a little story. You know it, but you didn't seem to get the point. When I'm through you're going to get up and walk out of here. One noise out of your mouth or one hesitation and you will need plastic surgery. Nod if you understand me."

I nodded.

"Good. Once upon a time an Army jeep ran over a private as she lay sleeping in her bag. She was paralyzed. The driver was joyriding. SOB number one. Now you would think the Army would be very concerned for her. Her commanding officer assured her he would deal justly with this situation. He lied. SOB number two. The driver was the son of a three-star general. Therefore the primary concern was containment. The woman was contained and silenced. Her objections and protests were lost in an administrative morass. She was honorably discharged just as fast as they could get her in a chair and out the door.

"One would imagine that a woman so grievously injured in the line of duty would have the support and respect of her family and friends. Her father wrote her a letter while she was in the VA assuring her she had a home with him. Unfortunately her father was a drunk. When she showed up he didn't remember writing that letter. He told her she had a few months before he sold the house and moved on. SOB number three. Her mother was institutionalized. She was the recipient of a lethal dose of early onset Alzheimer's. If you hadn't disappeared from your own mother's life you could have found out firsthand how richly rewarding it is not to be recognized by the woman who bore you.

"The strange part of this story relates to this woman's friends. The first week she was back home, they came by to let her know how much they cared. Then they faded away. No reasons were given, but one by one the intact, two-legged men and women whom she loved, laughed with, cradled through their trials, and danced with in their celebrations, they all found other places to go, and other people to be with. Did they think paralysis was catching? I don't know. But I do know they didn't want to be around a gimp. Maybe it was too depressing for them, too real or too sad. SOBs numbers four through sixteen.

"The woman found her own friends, most of them in chairs. She had three lovers, two men and one woman, two gimps and one normal. They left, too. Either they wanted to be taken care of by her, or they wanted to take care of her. Her strength cast an uncomfortable light on their own weaknesses, so they left. They weren't SOBs, just dissappointments.

"She decided intimate relationships were not worth the pain. A dog could give her far more loyalty, affection, respect, and companionship than any human could.

"She took one last shot at intimacy. Big mistake. After the first date, the guy almost drove off on his bike into the sunset. But he came back, and that counted for something. Then he lied to her about a not-so-ex-girlfriend. She knew he was never to be trusted. Sooner or later the lies would turn into betrayal. So she told him to get the hell out of her house, not to call, and to move damn quickly. Now get the fuck out of here, SOB number seventeen."

I left.

As I closed the door I heard her say, *"Braaf."* It means "good" in Dutch. It was her release command for Ripley. Her voice was weary.

CHAPTER NINETEEN

So what do you need, the gentle hand-holding or the rough stuff?"

This was not a sarcastic question from Rose. She had asked it one other time and I had answered, "Hand-holding." Her kindness has been all that had stopped me from putting the barrel of one of my pistols in my mouth. She'd held off the suicide sirens for two weeks until the lithium kicked in.

But tonight's cloud was not that dark. "Whatever. Balls on, Rose. I can take it, I guess."

Rose grinned. "So let me get this straight. In the last week you got shot at, pissed off the daughter of a Japanese gangster, almost jumped in bed with an old girlfriend, found out your mother died, connected up with the mother of your child, met her double in an angel store, lied to Sally, got dumped, had nightmares—including the recurring one about the guys you dealt with in the spring—and fell into a depression. You've decided that the depression is purely a biochemical event. All this, coincidentally just at the same time you decided to tell me your deepest, darkest secret. Do you think there might be some psychological connections here?"

"Can we go back to the hand-holding question?"

"Too late, Warren, you lost your chance. Come on, get to work. What's going on here?"

I ran my fingers through my thinning hair and sighed. "I prefer the physiological explanation. But, if you insist, I think maybe my past is overwhelming me. All this crap is coming back, and totally screwing with my present. All I want is to live a quiet, unobtrusive life. But I'm being roped into this bogus investigation, shoved at a daughter I never met, and surrounded by ex-girlfriends, now including the only one I care about: Sally. That's enough to depress a normal guy."

Rose nodded. "And we all know you're not normal. I think it's true. You *do* have way too much on your plate. I have a suggestion about what to take off that plate right now."

"Shoot."

"The secret about your past. I believe if you can offload that to someone, everything else might lighten a little. That's not to suggest you won't need your meds to get through this. But telling me that story will help the meds do their job."

I said, "You're just a voyeur, a collector of the forbidden, a miser of other people's suffering. You hate that I have something you don't know, don't you?"

"You're right, Warren. I do collect tragedy, sorrow, shame, guilt. I collect it by the barrelful. That's my job, and sometimes it makes me sick, or wakes me up in the middle of the night. I get paid the big bucks to haul out your psychic garbage. Now, look me in the eye and tell me that you have no part of you that needs to tell someone what really happened in the late sixties."

I looked at her for a moment. Then I said, "March sixth, 1970 to be exact."

Rose waited quietly.

I looked at my watch. Twenty minutes left. I would tell her the first chapter only.

I joined the weatherman after the Chicago Democratic Convention. Actually Veronique introduced me to the leadership. They loved that I had some ROTC experience, and knew my way around armament.

"A lot of shit happened after the convention. Pigs kept shooting Black Panthers. White revolutionaries got beat up and were jailed regularly by the man. We went back to Chicago to tear it apart in October of '69. We thought ten thousand supporters would be by our side. Instead, three hundred of us got our asses whipped repeatedly by the pigs. The FBI decided they could jail the lot of us on 'interstate conspiracy to incite riots.' But they had to find us first. By February of 1970 we all went underground."

I was back in Flint, that cold auditorium where we announced to the world our decision to disappear. We'd already ferreted out two FBI plants, and we knew there might be more. That weekend we culled our ranks in half, until there were only 150 or so of us. We split into three collectives: San Francisco for the least militant, just a few bombings now and then; Chicago/ Detroit and New York City, home of the real crazies.

We never wrote down any plans for any actions and made damn few phone calls. I was the Traveler. I kept my hair short.

I put a new engine and another hundred thousand miles on my VW van in five months. My job was to circulate from collective to collective to pass information around.

When a collective decided on an action, they would talk it over with me. Then I'd head off to the Weather Bureau, our central committee, usually based in Chicago, though sometimes it would move to one of the coasts. I'd get their okay and then head back to the collective with recommendations and a timetable. That way we could coordinate to cooperative outbursts of protest.

It was cumbersome, but it worked. None of us ever had a shred of evidence brought into trial documenting our conspiracy. There were no letters to read, no phones to tap. No evidence. That's because the FBI never got their hands on me. I could have sent seventy or eighty folks right into prison.

Veronique was pretty heavily involved with Paula, a cell member in New York. I didn't see her much, except for an occasional weekend when we would sneak off together. 'Q,' oh, that was my nickname for Veronique, anyway, Q didn't want anyone in Weather to know that she and I were an item. "Smash Monogamy" was one of our slogans.

In late February I was on the crew that planted a bomb in the house of Judge Murtagh, the bastard who was going after Black Panthers. No one was home when it went off. Then I headed out to meet with the Chicago cell. I got back to New York on the sixth of March.

We all lived in a New York City townhouse that belonged to Paula's parents, the chick that Q was so tight with. Her dad was a diamond importer, and was on a long trip to Europe and South Africa, so the New York cell had the run of the house.

We'd turned downstairs into the armory. When I was in town I would work with Frank, Ted, and Terry to design and manufacture explosives.

The afternoon of the fifth I called from Chicago and set up a council meeting of the Weather Bureau for Friday morning. I drove all night, got out of my van, and walked into the Greenwich Village townhouse to brainstorm about the Chicago cell's plan to bomb a police station.

The Weather Bureau meeting was a pretty good group: Bernadette was in from California, Diane, Kathy, Frank, Paula, JJ, Ted, and Terry were there. As usual, Veronique missed the meeting. She hated the political diatribes that those meetings could degenerate into. Later on, during our regular "Weatherfries" group confrontation sessions, she would have to do a "Cut Check" and then she'd get blasted for "lack of commitment to the movement." But she was sleeping with most of the commune so she got away with it.

The Chicago plan I presented had a few flaws. I told them that a bomb too big might take out an apartment building next to the station, possibly killing innocent families. Ted said, "Make the bomb big. That piss-ant firecracker we used on Justice Murtagh didn't hurt a fly. This is a war. The innocent sometimes must die alongside the guilty." I'd always thought of him as a moderate in our cause, but lately he was going over the top.

Veronique met me right outside the dining room as the meeting was disbanding. She whispered, "Go downstairs and look at the bombs. Then meet me under the arch." Then she walked out of the building.

Bernadette and JJ left as soon as the meeting ended. Frank went upstairs. I chatted for a little while with Kathy and Terry and then went downstairs. The bomb room was messier than I liked it. I was always stressing order and cleanliness when working around high explosives. Ted was at the table, taping together sticks of dynamite with electrical tape. I looked a little closer. Stuck through the tape were carpenter nails, the heads of the nails against the barrel of the sticks of dynamite, and the points sticking outward through the tape. I acted nonchalant. "Oh, we're branching out into antipersonnel ordinance, I see." Ted nodded without looking up. "These are for a special project. You have no need to know about them. If you're not going to help me out, please leave me alone. I've got work to do."

"Battery disconnected?" I asked. It was a thing I had drilled into them all to ask whenever they left the bomb room. We used D cells on our actual ordinance, but it was too expensive to keep buying batteries all the time just to test the wiring of the bomb detonators. So we used a car battery that we stepped down to the correct voltage. This was a pretty safe operation as long as everyone was extra-cautious about that battery.

"Always disconnected, now get the hell out of here, Traveler." He was in a foul mood today.

I walked over to Washington Square, in the heart of Greenwich Village. It was a crisp, sunny, spring morning. Kids were in school, moms were wheeling their strollers around, and a couple of people were actually smiling, a rarity for New Yorkers. Veronique, in a peasant blouse and bell bottoms, saw me and came out from the shadows of the arch. She took my arm and we began to stroll around the square, appearing like two old lovers. She smiled at me, but her voice was tense and low.

"Tomorrow they're going down to Fort Dix with those bombs you saw. They plan to blow up a dance. They figure at least a hundred sure kills. Richard, we're talking about a room full of young girls, out for a night of fun. Those kids have nothing to do with imperialism, Vietnam, or the Army. JJ, Ted, Frank, and Terry are out of control. Nobody can stop them. We've got to do something."

The next set of images flooded in, and the memories of that bitter smell. I couldn't go on. I opened my eyes, and left New York City, circa 1970.

I was back on Rose's couch. My throat kind of seized up. I looked at my watch. Ten more minutes. Not for me. I had to get the hell out of there.

"I'm going to stop now, Rose. I know you would be more than glad to give me an extra session right now. But I'm done. I'll see you next Wednesday at the usual time."

Rose said, "Tell it your way, at your time. I'm here whenever you need me. I will see you Wednesday, unless you need an appointment sooner. And Warren, thank you. I know this is one of the hardest things you have ever done in our work together. I appreciate how much trust it is taking for you to tell me this."

"Yeah, it sucks. See you Wednesday."

I was out of there.

CHAPTER TWENTY

Saturday flooded ruthlessly into my bedroom, ending another fidgety night. This morning the firing squad had new ammunition. "Warren, you paranoid idiot, the rest of the Weather Underground turned themselves in. And you know what, you sick fuck? Most of the time the cops didn't really care. Look around you, buddy. Mark and Bernadette are professors, John's a politician, Bill wrote a book about the underground and did a frigging book tour. And here you are, loser, still playing guerilla warrior. The sixties are long over, you foolish old man." I pulled up the covers and tried to go back to sleep.

When you live across the street from a clock tower, sleeping in is an unlikely event. When the carillonneur started playing Wagner, I knew there was no more rest. It was time for my fix.

The front table at Caffe Med, where I usually sit, was already taken, but I didn't mind sitting up in the balcony, removed from the riffraff. It took me two double lattes to remember that I had promised Edward to drop by and hear *Satan for Dummies*.

His temple was down in the flats, so I went back home to get my car.

Sacramento Street is as close as Berkeley gets to looking like Oakland. The four-lane street is flanked with thrift stores, liquor stores, abandoned gas stations, and empty lots enclosed by rusty chain fencing. It is a visual hymn from the underbelly of the American dream.

There was no sign on the clapboard storefront with the address Edward had given me. I parked, locked my doors, and walked up to the black door. As I got closer I saw a small brass sign on the door that read LEFT HAND PATH FELLOWSHIP HALL. Thumbtacked underneath it was a notice: "Informational Seminar: Saturday, 12:00. By invitation only." They certainly were keeping a low profile.

The antechamber was a small room with closed double doors facing the entrance. To the left side of the doors an attractive blond man sat at a table with a list of names in front of him. When I gave him mine he pressed a button under the table and I could hear the doors unlock behind him. "Go on in and sit anywhere. We will be starting in about ten minutes." I guess Edward was taking security seriously.

The inside didn't look like a church. Comfortably padded portable chairs were loosely arranged in rows, and there were armchairs and couches interspersed among them. The chairs faced a slightly raised dais on which sat one wooden chair, a small side table with a glass of water, and behind it a long bookcase. No stone altars, black candles, inverted crosses, or obsidian daggers anywhere in sight.

The audience consisted of about fifteen men and women, mostly men. No one met my eyes as I looked around. I guess

122

Satanism isn't chic in the East Bay. If this shindig had happened in San Francisco it would have been crawling with goth wannabes and reporters from the *Bay Guardian* looking for a cover story.

Edward came out in a sports jacket and slacks: formal wear, in Berkeley. He sat on the chair on the dais, took a sip of water, nodded to a couple of us, and then began.

"You were invited to this meeting for two reasons. One, you displayed an interest in the Fellowship of the Arising Night. Two, after interviewing you on the phone, we determined that you were not mentally ill. Congratulations." The crowd laughed.

"Mental illnesses are no barrier to Christian churches, particularly the kinds of psychopathology that lead to a blind obedience to authority, a fear of autonomy, and a rejection of intelligence. Actually those illnesses will stand you in good stead with just about any other religion. Those are the kinds of con- verts priests and ministers long for.

"We toss people out as soon as we unearth those passive, worshipful, compliant tendencies. As a result ours is a small but obstreperous congregation." Again there was a collective chuckle.

"I ask you to do one small favor. Banish from your mind all the collective Christian propaganda about satanists as animal killers, cannibals, child rapists, virgin defilers, or evil sorcerers. Never has one of those allegations been proven in a court of law. And that is simply because they are not true. Hate to disap- point you, but if you came here to despoil anyone, you'll need to find another venue." He was being quite charming.

"In a nutshell, here's what we believe. In one way we admire the Christian version of Satan. Lucifer was the only one in

Heaven or on Earth to oppose the cruel, capricious, and despotic dictatorship of Jehovah. However, the deity we worship is a much more complex entity than any fallen angel. Our Satan is a universal force that creates and destroys. He cherishes diversity and abhors uniformity. He made none of us in his image; instead he created each of us unique. He inspires each of us to discover our own power, exert our own will, trust our own ethics, and obey nothing but our own mind and heart.

"The meek may envy worshippers of Satan because we will not compromise our truth. The powerful will hate us because we do not submit to their authority. And most people ignore us, because the Left Hand Path asks too much of them. This path, leading into the darkness, asks that you discover your own deepest truths, instead of blithely accepting the watered-down ethics you learned in church and in front of your TV. It asks that you use your power and your force of character to fight for what you want. It asks that you punish wrongdoers and banish psychic vampires from your lives. It calls you forth to live out your passion, your sexuality, and your hungers instead of sacrificing them on the altar of respectability. Instead of sitting properly in uncomfortable pews on Sunday, we gather Friday nights to do magic and to celebrate our erotic aliveness.

"Are you looking for a spiritual path that honors your exceptional individuality rather than asking for your obsequious obedience? Are you seeking a way of life that demands you live fully today instead of gathering Brownie points for some mythical afterlife? Do you want mentors who focus on you harnessing the unknown depth of your personal power rather than pushing you to surrender into some cosmic soup of universal merging? If so, then you may have found a home."

I tuned out as Edward went into a lecture about Egyptian religions, Freemasonry, and the comparatively recent breakup of the Church of Satan. I wasn't a candidate for any religion. I couldn't see a lot of differences between an old man in white robes surrounded by angels, a satyr with goat horns and cloven hooves, or a blaze of universal light and love. All those images just seemed like products of frantic imaginations, teetering on the edge of chaos and desperately looking for some way to escape the inevitability of death.

Instead of paying attention to the lecture, I reflected back on all the data I had collected about these damn murders. I looked for some pattern in all this random noise: a sequence of perfect murders, an angel lady with a checkered past, a bullet fired at me, and an enticing and unwanted old girlfriend. I thought about Sally. No word from her in four days. I thought hard. Then I got a headache.

I didn't want to chat it up with Edward, or to convert. Besides, it was getting pretty stuffy and at least one of these potential converts didn't believe in deodorant. I got up and left. Hell, in a church that hated authority as much as this one did, walking out on the leader was probably worth a gold star.

Sacramento Street was baking. I headed for my car when I heard, "Stop dead, you motherfucker, or I'm wasting you where you stand!"

I kept walking, but I was smiling for the first time since I woke up. I heard the high-pitched screech of bicycle tire brakes and a man riding a mountain bike swung around in front of me and blocked my way.

125

"Yo, Mac," I said.

Officer James McNally was a Berkeley cop. Oddly enough he was also a friend of mine. A wiry little guy, he had steel-colored eyes and his brown hair was closely cropped. Today he was in spandex black bike pants, not those ridiculous Bermuda-shorts uniform that the Bike Squad wore. His Day-Glo orange tank top read SHIMANO XTR CRANKS.

"Hey, Tarotman, you're not working the Ave today. You want to go shoot this afternoon?"

Mac and I had originally met at a shooting range in Marin. We both loved our Kimber Team Match II .45s, and met about once a month to see who was the better shot. The loser bought dinner at Tandoori Chicken USA, a dive out in the boondocks that served awesome Indian food.

When I was in a depressed cycle, target shooting was one of the few activities that I excelled at. I didn't really care about my score. My nerves were slow, steady, and unattached. Give me the blues, and as long as I didn't turn the barrel toward my head, I was a damn good shot. I was going to kick Mac's ass. "Let's do it. I've got to go out and get my gun. See you at the range in two hours."

Rose had made me promise not to keep guns in my apartment. Impulsivity, depression, and live rounds of ammunition don't mix very well. I had a storage locker out in Antioch, paid for under another name. That's where I kept a stash of cash and my pistol collection.

I scored my best round ever, 180 out of 200. Any dork can do that with a .22 target pistol. But with a .45 that score surprised even me. Over my second tandoori chicken sandwich, I started in on Mac. "Look, Annie Oakley, I've got three things

126

to say to you. One, today pretty clearly demonstrates that you can't shoot worth a damn. Two, you keep bitching and moaning about how you hate your new lieutenant. And three, you're sick of biking all over Berkeley. Why don't you dump this cop shit and do what you want?"

I expected him to get in my face, but he didn't say anything for a long moment. Then he said, "You're right, Warren. I'm starting to hate it. But I've got to pay the bills."

"Bullshit. If money were no object what would you do?"

He knew right away. "Open a mountain bike shop for cross-country competitors and rich wannabes: with hand-built, custom fitted frames, and top-of-the-line equipment. I mean real quality: Chris King headsets, Manitou forks, Hope mini brakes, XTR derailleurs, Mavic Crossmax wheels, the whole nine yards!"

I had no idea what he was talking about, but I could see his gray eyes sparkle. I couldn't do much for myself right now. I was a failure as a detective, a loser as a lover, and a phony as a revolutionary. Maybe the best I could do for civilization would be to remove one pig from law enforcement.

"How much would it cost to set you up?" I asked.

"Knock it off, Warren. Your biggest bonus comes from your SSI check, have no idea what start-up would cost. But I can tell you one thing: Nobody's going to dump twenty or forty grand into an untried project run by a novice."

I said, "Mac, you're scared. Cut the crap, and put together a proposal for initial start-up and one year's operating expenses. I'll show it to a very rich tarot client of mine. Either that or shut up, stop whining, and work in your dead-end job until you retire and eat your gun."

He just looked at me, silent. Then he shook his head.

"Chicken?" I asked.

"Whatever. I'll think about it."

"Look, Mac, never mind. I know my client. 'I'll think about it' will never fly with him. He only finances the inspired or the desperate. He gave me the stake I needed to start my tarot business because I was going to kill some well-heeled Nordstrom's customer if I didn't get off the floor and out of there. 'Whatever' doesn't cut it. Give me your proposal when and if you ever really give a damn about your dream. If it's just a good idea, forget it. Okay?"

"Yeah, sure. See you, Warren." He walked away: his shoulders slumped, his head down. And I thought I was the one battling depression.

As I drove home the sun was near the horizon. It was almost finished punishing us. I wasn't feeling chipper, but at least making someone more miserable than I was had cheered me up a little. I was almost content.

I had no inkling that someone had been tailing me all day.

CHAPTER TWENTY-ONE

I had two calls to make before I could crash. I did the easy one first: Rev. Sharon Morrison. I got her answering machine. "Blessings to you. This is Reverend Morrison of the Church of Salvation in Christ. Today's reading comes from Revelations, chapter twenty, verse ten: 'And the devil, who deceived them, was thrown into the lake of burning sulfur, where the beast and the false prophet had been thrown. They will be tormented day and night for ever and ever.' Remember to live righteously and cast Satan out of your life. Please leave me a message of any length, and include your phone number even if you think I have it. Services begin tomorrow at ten. Go with God."

This sounded interesting. Reverend Mouse was definitely a contender. I felt a religious urge arising in me. Tomorrow was a good day to be saved, even if it had to be in Hayward.

No more putting it off. Now I had to call the mother of my child. Yuck! I walked down to the street, and this time picked the pay phone next to the pizza parlor.

"Hello?"

"Hello, Cathy."

"Oh, Richard. I'm so glad you called. I mean, I know you said you would, but I'm still glad you did. How are you?"

We chatted for about thirty more seconds until I started getting restless. Then I asked, "So have you had any thoughts about where we go from here?"

"Well, I don't know. I don't really know who you are. What do you think we should do next about me and Francine?"

I had to win her over. "Well, that's really your call, Cath. But I can tell you some things about me that might help you decide. I have a regular job. I've been in psychotherapy for years. I've done a lot of growing up since I fled from my old life. The reason I didn't contact you sooner was out of consideration for my sister's feelings. I wanted her to begin to trust me. She felt probably a lot like you feel: shocked, a little angry, and hurt. I'm trying to avoid harming anybody. So I'm asking you to decide based on what you think will cause the least harm."

I let the silence sit there. Then she said, "Well, okay then. I want you to meet Francine. And Justin . . . you haven't held your little grandson yet. He's such a dear. So, is it all right if I tell Fran about you? I mean she needs to know the truth, don't you think? Is that okay?"

"Yes, she does. But, if it's all right with you, I would like to be the one who tells her."

"Oh, of course. I totally understand. She is going to be amazed. Where do you live? She's in Santa Cruz, California. Is that anywhere near you?"

"Yes. I'll go see her very soon, if she wants to see me."

"Oh, she will. I know she will."

She gave me information I already knew from my investigations, but I acted like it all was new. Then she said, "This is a miracle."

"Yeah, I guess it is. Well Cathy, thank you for everything. If you ever need to reach me, just contact my sister and I'm sure she will forward the message. I wish you the best in your life. Good-bye."

"Oh well then, good-bye Richard. Be well. Call again if you feel like it. It's wonderful to hear from you."

"I will call you again, Cathy. I promise. Maybe after I visit Fran. Good night."

I could see her hanging up her retro princess phone and lying back on her pink silk coverlet. Maybe she would reach over and pick a small chocolate from the box on her Regency bed stand. Then she would thoughtfully rest it on her tongue, not biting down but letting it melt. While her mouth filled with rich sweetness she'd replay a sentimental and sanitized version of the story of our love. In that moment I was so glad I was a freak.

It was time for my own reflections. It had been a week since Mr. Hightower had asked if I believed in evil. My life had turned into a swamp since then. I kept thinking about all the things that had gone wrong in seven days. I had been blackmailed into playing detective, gotten shot at, lost my girlfriend, and I'd sunk into a rotten depression.

I couldn't sleep. I wanted to talk to somebody. I was lonely. I decided to send Sally an e-mail. After all, she didn't say anything about forbidding that.

```
Dear Sally:
Hey, don't get pissed. You can just delete
this, or hit reply and tell me not to write,
```

or send back a Trojan horse that wipes out
my disk drive. I'm just hoping you'll let me
keep this one thin line of communication
open. I don't expect a reply. Just let me
write every so often. Please, I won't inun-
date you, I promise.

News of the world: I found out why all
right-thinking people should become satanists today. Really, it was more interesting than I thought. Don't worry; I'm not
about to convert. My demons won't let me
worship someone else's.

Also, I talked with the mother of my
daughter. She was just as sweet as she was
four decades ago. No wonder I left. I like
tough girls. Though you do have the sweetest
smile in the world. I may go see my daughter
and grandson soon. That feels weird to type!

I'll go now. Thanks for reading this. I
miss you. Warren

I almost deleted it. It was so clingy. I sent it off before I could
destroy it. God, I needed to talk to Rose. Instead I lay back
down on my bed. For many hours I watched the immobile pattern of light and shadow that the streetlight cast across my bedroom ceiling.

CHAPTER TWENTY-TWO

Denny's at two in the morning was dead. There was a fat man worshipping his banana split, two cops eating quickly before their walkie-talkies went off, and a woman, alone at the counter, nursing her vanilla milkshake and writing in a red, leather-bound book.

I can still smell the smoke in my hair. When I get home I'll have to throw out all these clothes, right down to the bra and panties. I'll wash them at a Laundromat and then dump them. No evidence.

Thank God her appetite finally got the best of her. When she jumped my bones as I walked into that dirty log cabin, I thought for sure I'd have to make it with her before we could get to dessert. But I didn't want to play. She smelled. Not as much as she does now, though.

God, I played the modest but willing girl right to the hilt. I let her know that I wasn't going to be on the menu until after snack time. Then she was more than willing to let me prepare the appetizer plate. We didn't even need to get to the hot fudge sundae. She scarfed down those nuts in ten minutes. It was a bit frightening. They really are addictive!

She was barfing within a half hour. Then all I had to do was keep her away from the phone. It wasn't all that difficult. Once she was reduced to curling up on the floor, I was free to set up the "accidental" blaze.

The place couldn't have been set up any better. Lace curtains right next to the wood-burning stove. I'm surprised that tinderbox of a house hadn't gone up in flames before now. There were lovely kerosene lamps all over the place, and a half-empty can of kerosene in the pantry. I wasn't so stupid as to spread flammables around. That's too easy to spot. But I strategically placed the lamps and open metal container near the wall that would be the first to go when the curtains flamed. It would take longer this way, but we were so far out a mountain road that I had no worries about helpful neighbors.

It went off perfectly. She was in a coma or dead by the time I got my fingerprints off everything and made sure that the curtains had ignited the cross members holding up the roof. I walked outside, admired my work, got in my car, and drove off. In this weather that fire may hopefully start a firestorm. A clean kill. This one was a work of art!

She closed her journal and sat back on the bar stool. For an instant she saw Ella's body curled up on the floor. A small tear formed in her left eye. She quickly picked up a napkin and wiped it away. Then she looked around to see if anyone had seen her moment of vulnerability. Satisfied that it had gone unnoticed, she swallowed and then in a calm voice asked the waitress for her bill.

CHAPTER TWENTY-THREE

Sunday intruded into my bedroom, once again unremittingly bright and cheery. This was going to be one of those days when everyone else remembered how wonderful it was just to be alive. And I would feel like Cassandra, telling everyone not to trust that big horse. I booted up my computer just in case she wrote back AOL had headlines about some big fire down south. No reply from Sally.

Today I had to run the gamut from Jesus to Lucifer. It took me a while to choose my costume. I wanted to dress neatly enough to look respectful and yet still fit in with a working-class congregation. Green slacks, a subdued Italian silk short-sleeve shirt, and plain loafers did the trick. You could buy a similar-looking outfit at Target; only it wouldn't fit as well.

Hayward is the most unpretentious town in Northern California. It's a blue-collar town no boutiques, no gourmet ghettos, no open-air markets, or wine-tasting festivals. The town's flower is the carnation. It's closer to the heartland than to Hollywood.

I'm talking about the honest American Heartland, not some consumer-spun, cartoon-image, soft-focused commercial with three old white guys chewing tobacco on a porch watching the hay grow and talking about how Halliburton sure makes life better for folks like them.

In Hayward whites were a minority, only about one-third of the population. There were a hell of a lot of hard-working families, some gangs, plenty of drugs, and an active peace movement that dated back before Vietnam. And there were down-home local attractions: like Buffalo Bill's, where you could buy the best pumpkin ale in the country, or the haunted kids' park near the old swimming pool where you can still hear the giggling ghosts of kids murdered by their swim coach. I liked this town a lot. It was too poor to be phony.

The Church of Salvation in Christ was made out of concrete block. The sign in front of the dirt driveway read:

Then the Wicked One will be revealed, but when the Lord Jesus comes, He will kill him with the breath from His mouth and destroy him with His dazzling presence. 2 Thessalonians, 2:8

SERVICE EVERY SUNDAY AT 10. SUNDAY SCHOOL AT 9:45.

REV. SHARON MORRISON.

It was a little after ten, and in contrast to many other churches across the land, this parking lot was filled. I parked on the street and walked in. Unlike almost every other building in Hayward, this church had air-conditioning, and it was cranking full blast. No one dozing off for this sermon. The room was packed so I stood against the back wall. The windows along the side were gold-colored glass, and red glass bricks in the form of a cross were set into the concrete block wall in front of me. Behind a simple wooden lectern a small woman in robes was leading the hymn. To her left a man was playing a small electric organ, and to her right a six-person choir was backing up her clear soprano voice. The all-white congregation was heartily joining in, probably to keep from freezing to death.

The only thing that looked out of place was the row of men in the front pew: six guys in dark gray suits, with very broad shoulders. They were too well dressed. I noticed two more standing on either side of the church, scanning the congregation: double-breasted gray wool suits, royal blue ties with a white cross logo. They reeked of security. I guess I wouldn't have to worry about getting held up at gunpoint while I was standing there.

After the song ended Morrison launched into her sermon:

"Our reading today is from Mark, 14:30. You all know this story well. Jesus said to Peter, 'I tell you that before the cock crows twice tonight, you will say three times that you do not know me.' We all remember how fervently Peter swore loyalty to his savior, but, as we know, he did betray Jesus three times that night. Do not condemn poor Peter. *You* are not without sin!"

She really punched that last sentence, and you could feel the audience straighten up and pay closer attention.

"You all know what it is to suffer. Maybe not like Jesus on the cross, but we have all suffered. Some of you got laid off and you wake up in the night scared to death about how you're going to pay the bills this month. We're all getting older, and many of you fear ending your days in a huge, institutional, old-folks' warehouse, uncared for and alone. We know what it is to suffer."

The audience nodded and made sighing noises in agreement. If they'd been black they would have been shouting out, "Amen, sister!" They were quiet, but they were thinking it.

"And sometimes, in the dead of night we *blame* God. Don't deny it! You all know what I mean. You know, when it's two A.M., and we think everyone's asleep. When our fear and pain race around inside our heads, we ask, 'God, why? Why are you doing this to me? I've loved you, and given of myself to you, And in reply you have hurt me. You have deserted me. You have abandoned me. You have taken my loved ones from me. I want to know why?'

The room was silent.

"I've got to tell you, you are talking to the wrong person. Do you really believe that a God who is love would abandon you? Do you really think that a God who gave us his only son would bring you such misfortune? God only wants to welcome you into his kingdom.

"When you are staring at your bedroom ceiling asking, 'Why?' ask the one who is really responsible for your suffering. Say, 'Satan, why are you breaking my heart? Lord of Darkness, why are you draining my will? Prince of Lies, why are you telling me that God is dead and that I am alone?' "

She was on a roll now, and she had the congregation mesmerized. Me, too.

"God created us in perfection. Satan taught us how to sin. God pours his blessings upon us every day. The serpent of the Devil wraps himself around your hearts. We forget our Lord. And then we blame God for feeling abandoned.

"But I have good news for you. Satan's days are numbered. The Lord has closed his eyes to Satan's lies and blasphemies for a millennium. And that millennium is fast coming to a close. In your lifetime Satan will be vanquished."

She walked out from behind her lectern and just stood before us, showing her vulnerability and daring us to judge her. Two more of her gray squad got out of their seats and moved to the side of the church. "You think I'm crazy. You think, 'Oh, yeah, she's the preacher. She's got to say that stuff about triumph and salvation to keep us coming back every Sunday. But she's deluding herself.' She's naïve, simplistic, and a little too much of a fundamentalist."

"I believe that God is just. Call me naïve! I believe that Satan's pollution has poisoned our faith. Call me simplistic. And you better believe that I'm a fundamentalist! The fundamental goodness of man shall triumph over the lies of the Devil. The fundamental righteousness of God shall expose the slimy manipulations of the Dark One. And every blow we strike for moral truth is a blow to the heart of Lucifer."

She shook her fist, startling awake the overweight man in a polyester suit sitting right in front of me. "The Devil's minions have been with us for centuries. Terrorists from years past are once again arising to do his work. Today they are joined by a whole new flock of evil adherents. Take up arms, and fight the enemy wherever you discover him: in bedrooms, in schoolrooms, on the streets of our city, on the loading dock. Fight for the truth we all hold so dear, because victory is almost ours.

"When we are face-to-face with Satan, God will understand that we may need to reinterpret his commandments a little, in order to destroy wickedness. Violence in the name of the sacred is no sin, it is retribution!

"Our children shall live to see a world of purity, goodness, and deep, abiding faith because of the sacrifices we are making today. For their sake, fight with all your might for the Lord."

She should have gone into politics. Well, there was still time. And if I see her winning elections, I'm heading for Canada. Finally, I understood what happened in Germany in 1938.

There was a fierce energy running through the crowd. A part of me wanted to join them: to convert, grab a gun, and fight by her side. The bigger part of me got up and left the church as unobtrusively as I could. This woman was scary: charismatic, narcissistic, and manipulative. She fit the type Rose had talked about. I had no doubt she could kill anyone she decided was one of Satan's minions. If she knew that I was a tarot-reading ex-terrorist working for a cult that was a spin-off from the Church of Satan, I'm sure that my name could easily rise to the top of her list.

CHAPTER TWENTY-FOUR

It was time to travel over to the other end of the spiritual continuum. I needed to have a little chat with my new employer, and without his seductive sidekick in the picture. I called the number Edward had given me.

"Yes?"

"Hello, Edward of many names. This is Warren. I appreciated your lecture yesterday. Quite illuminating, or do you folks say endarkening? Anyway, I'm not yet ready to convert, but I do want to fill you in on the investigation so far. Without your sister, if that is possible."

"Ah, so Veronique is casting her fingernail-on-the-blackboard charms on you again, I see. Yes, a meeting is in order. Today is Sunday, and therefore as you can imagine, it is a profane day in my religion, an excellent day for discussing our business. Where shall we meet?"

"How about Rick and Ann's up by the Claremont?"

"Too busy on Sunday. This is the only time I regret that there are not enough churchgoers in this town. My choice is Inn Kensington on the Arlington. It has a shorter wait."

We agreed to meet in front of the place in an hour, plenty of time for me to ascend from blue-collars to silk scarves.

Edward said, "If you need to carbo-load, the plate of Santa Fe home fries should do the job. Otherwise their chicken-apple-sausage omelet is pretty good."

He was obviously a frequent customer. After I ordered, the waiter asked, "The usual?" Edward nodded. "What's the usual?" I asked.

"A double order of egg whites and vegetables scrambled in olive oil, unbuttered sourdough toast, and a fruit salad."

"That sounds very healthy."

"I am the oldest member of my family. Most of us die off in our thirties, from stroke or heart attack. Veronique and I are on borrowed time. We share a multigenerational combination of tiny blood vessels and an overdeveloped capacity to create plaque to clog those arteries and veins. It makes it very difficult to purchase life insurance. Giving up sugar was the hardest thing for me. I still dream about ice cream sundaes built over a base of hot fudge brownies."

I said, "I didn't notice much restraint in your sister's diet when we went out to dinner the other night."

"No, her approach is a little different from mine. I err on the side of hypochondria; she errs on the side of contempt. She believes that sheer cussedness can overcome any cardiac deficit. I hate her for her excess. Of course diet pills and purging probably help her to avoid my portly silhouette." He sighed. Then he said, "So tell me what you've discovered."

I filled him in on the cast so far: Miko and the Japanese mob, the angel lady with the juvenile police record, the fanatic preacher with the telltale signature. Rose's profiling. Then I gave him my perspective on the attempt on Veronique's life, which he had already heard about from the mare's mouth, so to speak.

Again I urged him to contact the police and let them take over the case. "Edward, I'm completely out of my depth, and there is no way I can stop another killing from happening, or catch the person who's behind all this."

He reached into the breast pocket of the sports jacket that he was wearing and pulled out another one of those fat envelopes. "Can you see to it that the three people you mentioned are put under surveillance?"

I had some recent experience with this. "Sure, but it's going to cost you. Surveillance on three people can go over a thousand dollars a day. Cops are cheaper."

He slid the envelope across the table. "Here is ten thousand dollars. Are you going to be able to come to our meeting? It's tonight at eleven."

"Maybe. I can't guarantee it. At the church?"

He nodded. I put the money in my pocket. In for a penny, in for a pound. I knew just who to contact for the next phase of the work. Maybe then I could relax and forget this mess for a while.

As I got up to leave, he said, "Warren, just a word of advice. Trust no one. Not even me. Everyone lies." On that cheerful note I walked out to my car.

145

I got home and booted up my computer. No reply from Sally. I wrote four e-mails to her. Deleted each one. Lay down in bed. Got back up every so often to check my e-mail. Andrea 3324 wanted me to know about a great stock opportunity. Victoria@canadacheapdrugs had some Vicodin to sell me. Jen@2hot2handle.com wanted to show off her new, hot, live minicam. Vsblonc offered me a degree from a prestigious, non-accredited university. But Sally was silent. I crawled back into bed and lost the rest of that day.

CHAPTER TWENTY-FIVE

I t was a hot Berkeley night. No cooling breeze off the water. No misty, low-hanging clouds. Too much light from a harsh harvest moon, and heat still rising from the concrete sidewalks. Sunday night but no one was sleeping. Winos on the corners. Dope dealers hanging out in front of liquor stores. Bands of teenage boys hunting for trouble.

I parked across the street from the church under a streetlight. I looked both ways to make sure the territory was relatively gangster-free. Then I set my Club, locked my door, and hustled across the street to the church. It was safer in a room full of satanists than it was out on those edgy, silver streets.

Edward was in the lobby to meet me. He handed me a black, hooded cape and said, "Put this on. This is a small meeting of the Inner Council. They know you are here as an invested outsider. Be still, watch, and leave when I tell you to, okay?"

"As you wish, boss."

He gestured for me to go into the main hall and walked off down a side corridor. I know he'd joked about no virgin sacrifices, but my stomach was still tight. What did I get myself into this time?

Opening the doors didn't help any. The chairs and the dais were gone. A dozen or so hooded, robed figures stood in a loose circle around a triangular altar in the center of the open space. In the middle of the altar a fire burned brightly in a wide metal dish. I looked up and saw the building had a skylight in the ceiling directly above the fire. Moonlight poured in from the opening.

As I approached the circle, the satanists shuffled aside to make a space for me. I looked around the circle. The hoods were pulled back, and I saw that I, too, was being examined. Pretty ordinary, friendly-looking folks. About three-quarters men, mostly in their twenties to forties. A sprinkling of elders. They didn't look like demon worshippers to me.

The slightly overweight woman next to me said in a commanding voice, "Welcome, Warren Ritter. Your work on our behalf is much valued. Your presence is appreciated tonight." A number of other heads nodded. I nodded back. Then all were silent again, listening to the crackling of the fire.

A door opened and two figures in red silk robes entered. Their hoods were thrown back. Around his substantial waist, Edward wore a wide black leather belt with a silver scabbard and sword hanging from it. Veronique's robe was split far up the side, highlighting her slender legs. Again the circle shuffled open, and the two hierophants strode up to the altar.

Veronique picked up a candle that stood at one point of the triangle, thrust it into the flames to light it, and then set it back down. She said, "We light the white candle to cast out the influences of Wicca covens, practitioners of white magic,

148

fundamentalist Christians, Catholics, and all other hypocritical followers of the light. May they stare at the sun until they turn blind."

The dark hooded figures all chanted, "We will prevail."

This was getting a little spooky. Veronique then walked over to another corner of the altar and lifted a candle that stood there. Again she lit it in the fire and said, "This is a night to be fully alive in our anguish and our fury. We have lost Richard Steed, a dear friend to us all. We light the red candle to ignite our passion and our will. Feel the power of this flame deep in your bowels. Our anger unites us and makes us strong. Tonight our circle shall concentrate our hatred and direct it at the murderer who threatens us."

Again the chant, "We will prevail."

Edward, already in front of the third candle, lit it. "The black candle represents the most powerful force in the universe: the Void. Darkness permits each of our tiny sparks of consciousness to radiate for the brief moment that is our life. Then it extinguishes us, and we are absorbed back into vast, unknowing silence. Darkness has many names, and we invoke them all."

He drew his scimitar. As he held it aloft the thin curved blade caught the flicker of the fire and shimmered in his hands.

"From the south we call upon Crown Prince Satan, Lord of Fire, and exposer of pretense. Come to us, tonight, enemy of orthodoxy, help us find and accuse the traitor who seeks to destroy us."

The crowd chanted, "Welcome, Satan."

He began to walk counterclockwise around the circle. "From the east we invoke Lucifer, bringer of enlightenment. Lucifer, use your blinding intelligence to help us pierce through the lies and

149

subterfuge. Unmask the cowardly assassin, and expose him or her to the searing heat of justice."

The chant arose, "Welcome, Lucifer."

He stood sword in air, almost directly across the room from me. The scarlet light from the fire made Edward's robe appear to be aflame. He called out, "Belial of the north, be here with us. Crown Prince of lust and power, strength and independence, kindle our passion for vengeance. Help us do unto this despoiler as he or she has done unto us."

"Welcome, Belial."

He strode to the fourth corner of the circle and said, "From the west we call forth Leviathan, the great black beast from the watery abyss. Come forth as an unstoppable presence and destroy this enemy utterly."

"Welcome, Leviathan."

Then he moved right in front of me, and pointed his sword down into the center of the fire. "We are servants of the dark, fanning our fierce, burning sparks as erotically and intensely as we can with every breath we take. We call upon the powers of the night to focus our intention, sharpen our will, and bring retribution down upon our enemy."

"We will prevail!"

Veronique reached under the altar and pulled out a burlap doll, about two feet tall with only the vaguest features of eyes and a mouth sewn onto its face. She placed it before Edward.

He turned and faced the cloth object lying before him. He spoke low, but so intensely that everyone in the room could hear him. "Our enemy does not yet have a face, a name, a gender. Stitched inside this doll are letters and messages from those who hate us and wish us ill. One of them is a murderer." Again he raised his sword and the flames seemed to climb up its silver length. "Now, focus all your loss and hurt, your rage and your pain on the tip of my sword."

I could almost see the streams of energy flowing from each person up to the point of his sword. I could feel the sorrow of losing a friend, and the fear. But all these were harmonics of the overriding emotion of fury, a ferocious desire to punish the person who had brought them this pain.

"Lord of Chaos, all we ask is an eye for an eye, and a life for a life." He drove the point down into the chest of the doll. He let go of the handle and the sword swayed back and forth over the impaled voodoo doll. Then he turned and faced me.

"Warren Ritter, you are our sword. Leave now and bring this fiend to a reckoning and help us heal our grief."

I nodded, turned, and walked out of the room. As I took off my robe in the antechamber I heard the beginnings of an atonal dirge. The words were in a language I didn't recognize, but you could cut the emotion of mourning with a knife.

CHAPTER TWENTY-SIX

V aldez Security, how may I help you?"

I had slept until ten. If I was going to be anyone's sword, I'd better sharpen up my act a little. I got dressed and walked down to the phone booth in front of Andronico's. I remembered that warm Latina voice. "Hello Isabel, it's Warren Ritter. Remember me?"

"Of course, Warren. How are you? Do you want to speak with Max?"

As usual, Max had been listening in. "Hello, Warren. What trouble did you get into this time?" I heard Isabel click off the line.

Max ran an Oakland security fiefdom. For the right price you could hire anything from bodyguards to spies. Maybe hit men, too, I don't know. He had deep connections within his community, and found work for many undocumented workers. In exchange for his largesse, his people provided information, surveillance, and protection for his clients.

Max believed that Hispanic workers were invisible in California. They could go anywhere and observe anything unnoticed by their white employers. Max's minions served the rich by cleaning their homes and offices, caring for their children, washing their cars, mowing their lawns, and seeing everything.

I told him about the murders. He didn't say much. He just interrupted once when I told him about Veronique getting shot at. "You be careful, Warren. You're not cut out to be a hero."

Then I told him what I wanted. "So here's the deal, Max. This is an all-cash deal. I need twenty-four/seven surveillance on three suspects. One is a student at Berkeley, one is a preacher, and the third a gift-store manager. I'll Priority Mail you the information and a retainer. This time no trouble, I promise."

I'd inadvertently been responsible for an unfortunate incident in which authorities took apart Max's office looking for a link to me. But he had forgiven me. He was a good friend of Sally's, so he cut me some slack.

Sally, Ripley, Heather, Max, and I got together about once a month to go to a flea market, or visit the dog park, or have a picnic. We were an informal family, one of the many that Max was a part of.

He said, "Give me their names and addresses and I'll start right now. But no written reports. You want to know what I know? You call me. And call from a public phone booth. There had better not be any problems this time, my friend, or this *will* be the last time."

I gave him the abridged version of what I knew about the three women. He didn't like Miko's connection to the Yakusa clan. "Look, Warren, I'm not putting my people at risk. Any problem with that target and I'm pulling my people. Understand?"

"Sure, I don't blame you."

Then he changed the topic. "Hey, I hear you and Sally are on the outs."

"I hope it's a temporary thing. Hey, Max, if you can put in a good word for me I'd appreciate it. I pissed her off, but I don't want to lose her." I wasn't very good at asking for help. But desperation can be inspirational.

"Sally's tough. You got to be tougher, Warren. Wear her down; she needs you. I gotta go now. You hang in there with that girl. She's worth it."

He was right. And I *was* going to hang in there with her. Still, that was no guarantee that she was going to hang in there with me.

I came back to my place and blew off cleaning the kitchen, my Monday chore. Instead I stuffed a big chunk of Edward's cash into a Priority envelope with a brief handwritten note, and headed off to the Northside Berkeley post office.

I ordered my latte at the French Hotel across the street from the post office instead of my usual digs across town. I bought a newspaper, and indulged in one of my favorite morning treats, cheese puffs. But the sweetness turned to library paste when I read a small box on page one.

DEVIL'S CULT MURDER?

A murder may have been uncovered when firefighters identified the source of the fire that threatened much of Santa Cruz County last week. Thanks to early detection and a massive statewide mobilization the fire was contained before it got out of control.

Tracking the fire back to its source, forest rangers found a

155

cabin belonging to Ella Fletcher burned to the ground. A body, later identified as that of the owner, was discovered inside. Ms. Fletcher listed her occupation as treasurer in the Fellowship of the Arising Night, a Berkeley sect affiliated with the Church of Satan. Suspecting foul play, the police ordered an immediate autopsy of the charred remains. Late last night in Santa Cruz, Police Chief Ed Rackris announced that the victim did not die from fire-related injuries. Homicide has not been ruled out.

(More on page 3.)

I knew this was going to happen. I didn't have very long to feel guilty. Before I could open my paper to page three my cell phone went off. It was Veronique, upset and pissed.

"There's been another murder disguised as an accident, and this one's very close to me. Ella Fletcher was the chief financial officer of our congregation, and she is . . ." She was unable to speak for a moment. I didn't know if it was rage or grief that stopped her. Then she said, "She *was* a dear friend.

"Tell me about her, if you can."

"She was a bit of a recluse. She'd disappear for weeks to her cabin in the Santa Cruz Mountains. She'd left my number with the Forest Service as the person to contact if anything happened to her. I got home after the ritual last night to a message that her cabin had burned to the ground, and the fire suppression team discovered her inside.

"This morning I just read that the fucking cops finally woke up. Now they know someone is trying to kill all of us. This is too much! Her death is going to leave the church in turmoil. I don't know what we're going to do. Warren, this killing has got to stop. I want this son of a bitch found!"

I said, "Son of a bitch, or daughter of a bitch, we don't know which. I've got the best detective agency in town trailing everybody we suspect. But I can't do much else. This isn't my profession, you know. You roped me into this. I think you need to call the police back and tell them everything you know. They're the ones who are going to catch this killer, not me. *Please* give them a call!"

She said, "You might be right. I'll talk to my brother. The pigs are going to come to us if we don't go to them. We might as well get this over with. Will you come and be with me when we talk with them, Warren?"

"No, I can't, Q. I have to keep a low profile. I'm trying to live here. Please keep my name out of all this."

"Sure, dear, I understand. I'll be in touch."

I still liked it when she called me "Dear."

CHAPTER TWENTY-SEVEN

All the way home I thought about murder. The deaths were getting more frequent and closer to me. I walked into my apartment and was hit with a wave of fear. I had something to live for! Too many of Edward's congregation were dying around me. I was their chief investigative officer. How long before the killer figured that out? Was the killer at that mass last night? Did he or she decide that I should be next?

Out of the fear came an unexpected resolve. I didn't want to spend my last breath in regret. I needed to meet my daughter, before it was too late! To hell with security, I picked up my home phone and dialed the number I'd memorized.

A woman's voice answered. "Hello?"

I so wanted to hang up. What the hell was I supposed to say? Well, I better say something. "Ah, is this Francine Wilkins?"

She was wary. "Yes? Look if you're selling anything I've got to go—"

Hmm, her father's patient temperament. "Wait, I'm not

selling anything. No free offers, no Hawaiian vacations, I promise! I'm an old friend of your mom's. From the sixties. I'd like to come and visit you."

"Why?" Patience *and* tact.

"I'm your father." On the other hand, I was such a smooth and considerate diplomat.

I heard the click as the line went dead. That line hadn't worked for Darth Vader, either. Oh well, it was a good idea. Maybe the next thing I could try would be to free climb to the top of the San Francisco Tower of the Golden Gate Bridge and see if I could fly. Instead I got up and headed to the kitchen for a soda. Before I got halfway there my phone rang.

It was my daughter. "Is this a trick?"

"Your mom has a small tattoo of an iris high up on her right hip. I was there when she got it in a tattoo parlor in Atlantic City. Her mother, Betty, slapped her across the face when she found out."

"Oh, shit. You are serious, aren't you? Goddamn Mom!"

Damage-control time. "Hey, easy, it's not her fault. I talked with your mom last week for the first time in decades. She had no idea that I was alive. She thought that I'd died in an explosion. Hell, I had no idea that *you* existed until this year. I asked Cathy's permission to call you, and I asked that I be the one to tell you. So, don't blame her."

"What do you want, money or what?"

Patience, tact, and trust. Somehow she had missed all the gifts her mother had to offer. Instead she had collected all of mine: edginess, bluntness, paranoia, and cynicism. A testimony to the theory of genetics. I liked this girl.

"I have plenty of money. I just wanted to let you know that

I existed, and to meet you, if you wanted to do that. Otherwise I'll leave you alone. Your call."

Long pause. "Meet me? Where?"

I said, "How about in front of the Giant Dipper." This is the huge wooden roller-coaster on the Santa Cruz boardwalk.

"When?"

"This afternoon at three?"

"Okay, I think that part of the boardwalk is still open. If this frigging heat breaks and the fog comes in I'll be in a purple scarf. Otherwise I'll be wearing purple shorts. I'll wait ten minutes, that's it." She got my impulsiveness, too. This was going to be interesting.

I said, "I'll be there, Ms. Wilkins."

"Hell, you're my damn father. I guess you can call me Fran. But I sure as hell won't call you Daddy. What's your name?"

"Warren, Warren Ritter. I changed my name. Your mom knew me as Richard. Say hello to her when you call her to check me out. I'll see you this afternoon, Fran."

"So long." Click.

Talking to Francine had punched a small hole in my emotional gray-cloud cover. I was going to exploit it. It was time for the ultimate antidepressant. Beyond caffeine: speed!

I was driving Highway 17 with its poorly banked curves, backed-up traffic, and daily traffic accident. A dreary, boring ride in a Honda Civic. My daughter wasn't going to see some middle-aged loser show up in his Japanese beater. She needed to know who her dad really was.

I puttered my Honda over to Alfredo's Cycles. He babied my

red Aprilia RSV Mille motorcycle. It had a 998 V-twin and more raw power and sex appeal than ten Ducatis or a thousand Harleys. As usual, it was tuned, gassed up, and ready to ride. Al knew that this was my escape vehicle. He kept it ready for me at all times.

I pulled on the leathers that he stored for me. Then I switched my wallet with the one in Al's safe. This one had a license and credit cards for David Ellbruck, the registered owner of this bike, a resident of Spokane, Washington, who just happened to have my face and birth date. I plugged my Motorcom helmet into my portable CB and police-band scanner and I was ready to ride.

There is nothing like the experience of wrapping your legs around a bike that can outpace any other vehicle on the road, period. Sure a Lamborghini is faster on a straightaway, but give me three tight curves and I'll leave it in my dust. Nothing on two or four wheels could touch me. Tangoing from lane to lane, I threaded my way through San Jose, and up into the mountains. No Smokies, and the road was clear. I made it to the boardwalk with time to spare.

Santa Cruz lived off tourists like a well-groomed vampire. In the eighteen hundreds, it sold San Franciscans baths in the healing waters of the San Lorenzo River. Then the big bands played their hearts out at the Coconut Grove. Finally, they managed to preserve the last decent boardwalk left on the West Coast. No gambling, no hookers, just good clean fun in what was then one of the most conservative cities in Northern California.

Then the university came in, the feminists ran out the Miss California beauty pageant, the progressives took over the city, and an earthquake flattened downtown. The town almost went broke and the boardwalk became a lifesaver, still drawing in sun worshippers willing to throw money around.

Back in the twenties, Charles Looff came into town and carved the fantastic horses, tigers, and griffins that made up the Santa Cruz carousel. I'd been there once, back in the sixties, and had caught the brass ring while whirling around to the music of the huge automated organ. Instead of handing it in for a free ride, I carried it around for years. I lost it off the coast of Alaska when I toppled into high seas from a fishing boat. I still occasionally missed the feel of it in my pocket.

I walked past the endlessly circling wooden animals and headed down to the Giant Dipper, one of the last boardwalk roller-coasters left. People think that a great ride requires lasers, virtual reality, 90-degree sheer drops, or reverse spirals tight enough to make you puke. I stood in front of an eighty-year-old statement that all it takes is some lumber painted red and white, a rickety, five-cab train, and a clanking chain.

I spotted her from a distance, walking toward me on the nearly deserted concrete walkway. The fog was lurking just off-shore so she had on both the grape-colored shorts and a scarf. She had my pre-cosmetic-surgery Jewish nose, my hazel eyes, and her mother's full lips and her own long black hair streaming out behind her.

She came up to me, no smile, and said, "Are you Warren, formerly known as Richard?"

"The same."

We stood there sizing each other up.

She said, "You don't look like Aunt Tara."

It bothered me that this woman and my sister had known

each other longer than I'd known either one of them. I said, "You look a lot like my mother."

"I know. Tara showed me some pictures."

Another long pause. Then it was my turn to try and keep this conversation going. "I'm not sure what I'm supposed to say. 'How are you?' seems a little lame. 'Who are you?' is too hard to answer. How about, 'Can we go get a cup of coffee somewhere?'"

She said, "No. I don't know how long I want to be with you. I mean, I know you're my dad, but really you're just some stranger who has eyes the same color as mine. We don't have anything in common other than that. Besides, I don't have that long to chat about life with you. My friend is watching Justin—you know I have a son, right? (I nodded.) My husband is off shift in half an hour, and I need to get back home. I think I should just shake your hand and leave, and call it a day."

I make a living reading people. Any honest tarot card reader will tell you the job is much more about acute observation than about any so-called psychic powers. Your client tells you what she wants to hear by her body language, and then you give her what she wants. This client in front of me didn't want to run off. But she didn't know how to come up with a good enough reason to make her stay. I could help with that.

"Sure, Fran, that's one option. We don't know what to do with each other, and just splitting keeps both our lives a lot less complicated. I have no idea how to relate to a daughter. I don't have any other children, and I'm not planning on having any."

Agreeing with her took a bit of the wind out of her sails. She hunched up her shoulders and took in a breath. I guessed she was getting ready to deliver the good-bye speech.

I jumped in, "Of course, then you'd never find out some things about yourself."

She bit. "What could you possibly know about me? You never laid eyes on me before."

I said, "You're right. But I know me. And, like it or not, there is some of me in you. I'll make you a bet. I'll tell you something about yourself that you haven't told anyone else. If I'm right we go for coffee. If I'm wrong I'll get on my bike and ride off over the hill. Deal?"

"Counter-offer. If you're right I'll give you a call someday, and we can talk over the phone. I really *do* have to be getting home soon."

"Deal." I looked at her, not having the slightest idea what I was going to say. That impulsiveness cropping up again. Well, let's hope there's a strong genetic component to my mood disorder. Here goes.

"Fran, you're getting worried. It's been three months, and you can't quite shake off that postpartum-depression thing. You don't want to take any medication because you're breast-feeding. Besides, every so often you wake up feeling like a million bucks. But sooner or later the blues creep back. You've been trying to hide it because you're ashamed of it. After all, this is supposed to the most precious time of your life. But too often these days, life just sucks."

Bingo. Her pupils dilated. She became a shade paler. Then she said, "How did you . . ." Then silence.

I said, "That's an unfortunate part of me that you've got inside your psyche. I can teach you a lot about how to manage it. But don't hope that it's going away anytime soon."

She shook her head, looked down at her watch, and said,

"What's your damn number? And don't expect a call anytime soon."

I gave her my cell number and didn't ask for hers. She needed to feel she was in control. Then she turned and stalked off down the boardwalk. I watched her turn the corner. There goes my daughter. What a bitch! What a kick!

CHAPTER TWENTY-EIGHT

She was pissed.

The heat wave finally broke. The wind shifted. The Sacramento Valley heat was sucking the fog in from the Pacific; the thick, cold fogbank blanketed the Bay Area. The lamps that lined the Berkeley Wharf could barely poke a hole in the grayness.

The intense, repeated crack of high heels hitting concrete woke the nighthawk who was resting atop one of those light posts. He looked up and down the wharf, trying to spot whatever it was that was making that persistent noise. Almost right below him, he saw a two-legged emerge from the mist, striding toward him. He felt some sort of unspecified danger in the animal's walk. He beat his long, gray wings. In an instant, he was invisible in the mist.

"Damn, damn, damn, damn," she cursed aloud. She was so furious that all she could do was walk as hard as she could, hoping to discharge a slight bit of her intense rage. She was furious. What the hell were those goddamn cops doing ordering an autopsy so soon? And who was this medical examiner? Speedy Gonzales? "No smoke in the lungs, so we suspected foul play." And why the hell didn't that fucking fire char that bitch to cinders? Besides, how the hell was she supposed to know that you could still detect poison in a charred, fucking corpse?

"Damn!"

And then, between one step and the next, it all drained out of her. The flaming reproach, self-hatred, and fury that she had been battling with all day dissolved. She slowed her pace, and took in a deep breath.

She remembered. She was the she-wolf. She was in charge. She was in control. She was above all the petty bullshit of domesticated animals. The guard dogs could sniff around all they wanted. They would find no trace of her. In fact, it was time to lay down a false trail, so they would go sniffing off in the wrong direction. She had one more sheep to slaughter.

What's done is done. Now it was time for damage control. She knew sooner or later that the cops would catch on to her little amusements. So she had to move into endgame a little early. No problem. My will be done.

After the next job, she could head back to Mexico City. If she timed everything just right she could be there in time for the raucous Mexican Independence Day celebrations. Only one more murder, and this one required very little prep time. After that, fiesta!

CHAPTER TWENTY-NINE

I woke up from the weirdest dream. In the dream, I realized that I was wrong. Philip was the killer all along. I had him trapped in a mill. The stones were grinding the wheat, the wide wooden paddles were cutting through the water in the sluice. The wooden gears were making a big racket. Philip was up on the second floor. I was climbing the stairs toward him. He stepped out, pointed my Kimber .45 at me and said, "Pay Attention, Richard!" Then he pulled the trigger. I heard a *pop,* and a flag came out of the barrel with the word BANG! on it. I knew in that instant that I finally had the answer right in front of me. Then I woke up. I lay there for a long time, but I couldn't make any sense out of the dream at all.

It was cold in my apartment. I got up and walked over to the window. Didn't see much. The fog had come in overnight and it didn't look like it was leaving anytime soon. Now everything was gray. I should be happy. I went back into bed and pulled up the covers. Who cared.

Finally I couldn't pretend that I might go back to sleep any longer. Crawl into wrinkled clothing, then just like I had the previous two mornings, check my e-mail. Nothing from Sally. I didn't want to be too pushy, but it had been three days. I'd send her another e-mail tonight. That was about all I had to look forward to.

I did my token gestures to enlightenment: five minutes of meditation, five minutes of yoga, and the short version of the Serenity Prayer: "God grant me the wisdom and courage not to kill myself today." Then I cleaned the bathroom, took my meds, and headed out for coffee.

There were a lot of reasons to miss Sally. Way down on the list, but still significant, was the way it blindfolded my "investigation," (if you deigned to dignify the clumsy wandering around I'd been doing by calling it an investigation). Sally could just hack into the police database and give me the latest update.

I felt half blind having to rely on the conjectures and inventions of the Oakland paper. The poisoning of Ms. Fletcher was still front-page news, with lots of teasers about how the perpetrator was just on the verge of being nabbed, and no hard news. I didn't know what the poison was, how the fire was set, or have any indication of the time of death. Just lots of rehash about the Church of Satan, and retelling of other grisly murders that have occurred in the Santa Cruz Mountains.

Wham! A stack of papers were slammed down on my table. I jumped. It was Mac, my favorite cop, but in civilian clothes and with a lovely bruise covering the right side of his face, dark grape around the edges and a center of pure vermilion.

I said, "I told you not to try and kiss a horse's ass."

"Not amused" doesn't even begin to describe the expression

on his face. He looked through his bloodshot eyes at me. This boy had been seriously roughed up.

I apologized. "Sorry, Mac. What happened?"

He said, "A doctor on his cell phone making a right hand turn in his Lexus SUV ran right over my bike. Unfortunately, I was riding it at the time."

"You're lucky you're still alive."

He nodded, and then looked down at the papers he had so loudly delivered. "Here it is. I've been working on it all night. What do you think?"

I looked at the top sheet as he stood over me. "Market Plan for the Outfitting and Launching of Epic Thrash: A Bike Shop for the X-tremely Demented." I glanced down at the first item on the initial inventory lists: "5 Ibis Bow Ti's, at $6,700 each = $33,500."

"I like your style, Mac. You really want to do this?"

"Look, Warren, the way it's going, I've got no future as a cop. I didn't join the force to catch the bad guys, or to make the world a better place. I took the job because it sounded exciting. Well, it's lost its luster.

"They took me off bike patrol. I'm assigned to support homicide P.M. shift, which I hate. After I get patched up, I'll try to get back on the bike squad. If I don't make it I'll end up behind a desk typing up endless field inquiries. Then, like you said, I'll retire at fifty and eat my gun at fifty-one. If I do make it back on wheels I'll end up crushed flat by the next fucking SUV. I'd rather die in the saddle of my V-10 Dorado flying down some slickrock in the desert, screaming with joy and terror, thank you very much. Warren, will you take this proposal to your rich client?"

I said, "He's a bit of a recluse, but I'll see what I can do. No promises. He may hate the idea."

"I'm not asking for a guarantee. Just deliver the message, okay?"

I smiled. "Okay, dude. Now go home and take a long, hot bath."

"I'm gone. And thanks, Warren. I really appreciate this!"

"Go!"

I'd have him in his shop by the end of the month. I loved the idea of deprogramming a cop.

I went back to reading last week's *Express,* the Berkeley free newspaper. I didn't get very far into an exposé of scams involving live-in lofts, when interruption number two bombed in. This one was a lot better looking.

"Hey, Warren, wassup?"

Heather plopped down in the seat next to me. She had on torn blue jeans, running shoes, and a black T-shirt that had a cartoon of a toddler dodging a harpoon and the command, BOYCOTT BABY OIL. STOP THE SENSELESS SLAUGHTER!

"Wassup yourself, girl. I haven't seen you for over a week. How's your bones?"

"Hanging loose, which is more than I can say for Sally. Hey, what's going down between you two? She freezes up when I mention the *W* name."

I'd always been straight-arrow with Heather. "I fucked up, girl. I went on a date with an old girl friend and didn't tell Sally until later. Not that anything nasty happened, except getting shot at. Anyway, Sally felt betrayed, and she aimed Ripley at me and told me to get out fast, so I did. I'm not supposed to call her or show up on her doorstep or anything. But I sent her an e-mail. No answer yet. How is she?"

Heather shook her head. "Like ice, like fire. Edgy as shit. I'm going backpacking with some buds, just to give her space. She is not healthy for children and other living beings right now. Poor Ripley."

"Heather, I'm not very good at asking for shit, but can you help me out here?"

"I don't know, Warren. You should have heard Sally bite Max's head off when he suggested that she chill a little and give you another chance. It wasn't a pretty sight."

It felt good that Max had tried. To take on the wrath of Sally meant he was a good friend.

I said, "I don't want to put you in the line of fire. I guess this is my problem to deal with. Thanks, anyway."

Heather put her hand on my arm. "If her panties are still in a wad when I come back, I'll give it a try. Hang in there, Warren. Why don't you call her?"

"Not a good idea."

Heather frowned. Somehow that last response bugged her. She said, "You know, Warren, for her to hate you so vehemently, she must really care a lot about you. She'll come around eventually. Just be there when she does. Don't even think about driving into the sunset, or she will be out of your life forever. No flight bag, got it?"

"I got it, I got it. My rambling days are through. I'm sticking this one out, don't worry. Where you going camping?"

"Lost Coast, up in Northern California. Perfect timing, huh? No sun, cold wind, mist, maybe even rain. Oh well, it's better than hanging around Sally. I've got to get out of here, I'm going to be late. I just dropped by when I saw you in the window. Love you, Warren. Aloha, bro!"

"I love you, too, Heather. Maybe I'll see you Sunday."

"Yeah, maybe at Sally's. Later."

She gamboled out the door, and left a sad, empty space behind her. I wasn't used to missing people, and I missed her already.

CHAPTER THIRTY

To stave off the loneliness, I decided it was time for me to play Sherlock. I stopped at a pay phone just off Telegraph and called Max.

"Valdez Security."

"Hi, Isabel, is the man in?"

"Hi, Warren." It was Max, listening in. "I've got a few pages of detailed surveillance reports, but I can distill it down to one sentence."

"Before you do, I just want to thank you for saying a good word on my behalf to What's-Her-Name."

Max laughed. "That Heather's been shooting off her mouth again, hasn't she? Yeah, well, my friend, I did what I could. Didn't make a damn bit of difference. You got one mad hen there, Warren!"

"Tell me about it. Okay, what is your one-sentence summary?"

"Two words, actually. Be careful. I've completely pulled surveillance from Ms. Tashima. Last night three men drove up to her house, men who I know to be extremely dangerous. I do not want my people to be witnessing anything having to do with Japanese gangs.

"And Warren, that's not the end of it. I had to pull surveillance on Reverend Morrison for a couple of hours. The first guy got blown the first day. A couple of well-dressed thugs in gray suits and blue ties told him to move on, and not to reappear anytime this year. No harm. I got a woman inside who has the situation under control. Just wanted to warn you, your minister has a very loyal and savvy following.

"Unfortunately we're three for three. Your suspects make us look pretty bad. The angel lady was the worst. We can't keep a tail on her. She's made us. She is damn sneaky. She knows some pretty good tradecraft. Where'd she come from?"

"Good question, Max. I want to find that out. Don't worry, I'll be careful. I understand about Miko. Do your best to find out where the other two go."

I decided to leave Miko alone for a while. She scared me. I was willing to leave Gracie to Max. If she was dodging Max's people, she was out of my league.

But what did this preacher lady have to hide? What did she need storm troopers to protect her from? I didn't have Sally, so I'd have to do my own hacking. I headed home, and entered "Rev. Sharon Morrison Church Salvation Christ" into Google, and got a lot of crap. Pictures of her installation six years ago, including photos of the reception in the social hall. On the Web page of the church I found texts of several sermons as fiery as the one I had witnessed, links to photo albums of both the all-you-can-eat bowlathon and the ice cream social fund-raising events, a long description of the preschool, stressing how essential early education was for making your children Satan-proof. Nothing biographical about the good reverend.

I tried just "Reverend Sharon Morrison" and hit pay dirt. Halfway down the third page was a link to an excerpt from a chat room that read, "Reverend Sharon Morrison may claim to be God's voice box, but if my brother Vic was still alive he would tell you a very different story!" The sender was Joey2332@aol.com. Good news, I too was a member of the closely knit community of AOL users. I looked under the member directory and read this:

Name: Joey Ballentino

Location: Michigan

Gender: Male

Marital Status: Divorced

   Hobbies and Interests: Fly-fishing, hunting, Civil War reenactment

Favorite Gadgets: GPS

Occupation: Sales Manager

I whipped off an e-mail: "Dear Joey: I am investigating Rev. Sharon Morrison, and I understand that your late brother had some information about her. Is there any help you can give me?" I gave him all my contact information: one of my cell phones, my house line, and my voicemail.

I went back online to see what else I could find, but two minutes later my cell went off.

The guy had a thin, high-pitched voice. "I'm Joey Ballentino. You just sent me an e-mail about my brother. Who are you, what's this about, and how did you get my name?"

Lying time. I put on my FBI voice, low and authoritative. "Hello, Mr. Ballentino. My name is Warren Ritter, of Valdez Security Services. Thank you so much for getting back to me so quickly. I'm a private investigator, and I am looking for sources who may have information about Reverend Morrison. I understand your late brother had some contact with her."

"You don't know very much, do you?"

Okay, I was going to have to get folksy. "Reverend Morrison has been less than cooperative in assisting us in this investigation. So far as I can tell she popped out of the earth in California six years ago."

"What's this investigation about?"

Hey, I was supposed to be asking the questions. But I needed this guy on my side so I said, "Look, Mr. Ballentino, I can't tell you all the details. Client confidentiality and all that. But it has to do with the reverend's abuse of her power, I can tell you that much."

"You better watch your own ass, Mr. Ritter. This is a dangerous woman. I think she had my brother killed. The police call it an automobile accident, but Vic was a top-notch driver."

I was close to landing this fish. "You know, what you say doesn't surprise me that much. There are a string of unsolved crimes out here in California that point in her direction. Why do you think she killed your brother?"

Joey said, "They were married for three years. Then he got creeped out by her and walked out. She divorced him in a snap. But then he started going around telling the truth about her, and I think she shut him up, permanently."

"Do you have any proof?"

"No, she's good. You want the goods on Sharon, talk to her mom. Elsie Morrison hates her daughter."

Life is sweet! "I think that's an excellent idea, Mr. Ballentino. Do you have that number?"

Calling Mrs. Morrison gave me more vitriol than I ever wanted.

"My daughter is a selfish, self-centered psychopath who will destroy anyone who gets in her way."

I love a gal who doesn't mince her words. Elsie Morrison didn't really care why I wanted to investigate her daughter. She just wanted to dish some dirt. "Sharon ruined her father's life with baseless, disgusting accusations. She drove her brother right into the hands of those communists. She murdered her husband when he started telling the world what a witch she was. She's a compulsive liar and a thief. The idea that she can pass herself off as a Christian is a joke. I'd like to beat some Christian values into her slippery hide. I hope I never speak to her again!"

Elise didn't stand a chance of winning the Mother of the Year Award. As much as I wanted to nail her daughter, this woman gave me the creeps. "Do you think she's capable of murder again?"

That shrill voice, claws on the blackboard, "Are you kidding? She'd do anything to get ahead. If there's money involved she'll steal you blind, and then blow your head off. You can't turn your back on her for a minute!"

Her vitriol was hard to listen to. I just wanted to get away from this lady. Luckily she beat me to the punch, "I'm sick and tired of talking about my daughter or even thinking about her. Good-bye, and don't call me again!"

179

Ten minutes later I was getting ready to head out for lunch when my house phone rang. I said, "Hello?" and a man asked, "Warren Ritter?"

"Yes."

Click. This was not a good sign. Someone had just back-tracked me. I tried to "star 69" them, but the call couldn't be traced.

Sherlock retired. I'd gotten a few more tidbits, but nothing to ring my chimes yet. I ordered take-out Chinese and settled down with my current book, *Night Flight,* by Antoine de Saint-Exupéry.

Almost midnight. No e-mail from Sally. I figured I had waited three days since my last one. That showed I wasn't being pushy. Tonight I could send out another one. Hell, before this happened, we used to talk every day.

Dear Sally:
Thanks for not sending back my e-mail. I re-aly appreciate you allowing this one line of communication to stay open.

First a quick update. I didn't convert to the Church of Salvation in Christ, although Reverend Morrison could make Hightower a de-voted follower. She's a Christian Hitler when it comes to mesmerizing public speaking.

Also, I met my daughter in Santa Cruz. She doesn't know what to do with me. Feeling is similar. Ball's in her court. Hmmm, seems that way everywhere.

Now, about us. Look, I know that your reaction to me wasn't just because I was
sneaky about Veronique. I know it's got to
do with a lot of things: things like my plan
to flee to Alaska earlier this year. And it
has to do with my flight bag. And my three
identities. Hell, I wouldn't trust me, if I
didn't know me so well.

This relationship stuff is hard for me.
Mostly I've lived a selfish life, doing just
what I wanted to do and living with the con-
sequences. I'm not used to taking other people's needs into account. Which is not me
trying to come up with an excuse. What I did
was wrong. It's just me asking you to hang
in there, while I learn how to do things
right. I promise never to make the same mistake twice.

I miss you, Warren

CHAPTER THIRTY-ONE

Blame it on the blues. Ordinarily I am fairly alert, perhaps even with a tinge of paranoid hypersensitivity. But Wednesday I had to fight my way through five tons of treacle to make it up to consciousness. I ached. I felt like I hadn't slept. I kept trying to forget my dream of champagne corks popping out of their bottles and then, like tiny cruse missiles, chasing me all over London. The depression felt like a serrated knife in my diaphragm, slowly sawing back and forth.

The weather was finally in sync: damp, chilly, and dismal. Again, I blew off my chores. I set out for the nearest supply of French roast. I stumbled out of the apartment door and turned right without being anywhere near my body. Behind me I heard a man's voice say, "Warren Ritter?"

I spun around and almost bounced off of the chest of one of the two gray-suited, blue-tied church hoodlums right behind me. As I grabbed him, trying not to fall over, I felt his shoulder holster under the jacket. Great.

He reached over to catch me. Then in a very smooth move he stepped between two parked cars, keeping me off balance so that I was almost hanging on his arm. He swept me past an open car door and into the rear seat of a dark sedan. He slammed the door behind me and I heard the automatic lock click. As the car jerked forward up the hill I fell back against the seat.

The windows were smoked, as was the partition between the front and the backseat. I had decided to take off my shoe and pound it against the window, in hopes of getting a pedestrian's attention when suddenly the car braked, backed up, and stopped. The partition lowered into a compartment behind the front seats.

Sitting in the passenger seat was a man dressed, oddly enough, in a gray suit with a blue tie that had a white cross embroidered on it. He turned around to face me. He was holding a very substantial Smith and Wesson Sigma 9mm pistol. He had my attention. In my peripheral vision I could see we were parked in a wooden garage. So much for any rescue fantasies.

I said, "Can I help you?"

"You've been investigating Reverend Morrison." He spoke with an Eastern, prep-school accent. His crew cut was a lighter gray than his suit. His eyes were olive, and his features fine. He didn't have the linebacker physique of his contemporaries. I imagined I was speaking to the team leader.

"I have?"

"Think this through, Ritter. I'm not in the mood for disposing of bodies. You called her mother yesterday."

Busted. They must have her phone bugged. Her Holiness Morrison was extremely thorough. You don't get this level of protection from ice cream socials and bowlathons. Where was her money coming from? And how could I get out of this garage alive? That was a much more pressing question.

"Yes, I did call Elise Morrison. Could you put that gun down?"

The barrel continued to point at my torso. Ducking was not an option.

He said, "Ritter, don't be a donkey's patoot. Listen carefully. I want you to end your investigation of Reverend Morrison right now."

Donkey's patoot? He didn't pick up that phrase on the lacrosse fields of Lawrence Academy. Where was this guy from?

I said, "Okay, consider it ended."

He smiled. It was not a warm smile. "Good. Now get out of the car."

I heard the lock click. I opened the door and got out with great alacrity. The passenger window slid down and he put his head out. I decided not to kick out and try to break his neck. He just might be faster than me.

"Ritter, one more thing. Come here."

I bent over to talk with him. I barely detected the motion behind me. Oh, an accomplice. Something crashed against my skull, suns exploded in my eyes, and that was all.

The headache was unspeakable. It kept my eyes squeezed shut for a very long time. Gradually I risked slitting open one eye. I was on dirt, in the shade. Then both eyes shut. I could smell diesel fuel. It was making me sick. I risked opening another eye.

I was on a dirt floor, face lying in an old oil spill. I rolled over. Really bad idea.

It took about an hour to make the endless three-block journey back to my apartment. Like I said, blame it on the blues.

CHAPTER THIRTY-TWO

Here are the ground rules, Rose. I tell my story and then I split. No questions about my appearance. No commentaries or interpretations about my story. Nothing from you, okay?"

I had no intention of telling Rose about my assailants. She'd just say I should go to the police. Besides, I had bigger fish to fry.

This was a Wednesday-night therapy session like no other. I was about to speak about the secret that I had sworn to myself would go with me to my grave. The setting couldn't have been filmed by Hollywood any better. The bloodred sun painted the clouds above it in shades of magenta and orange. The light turned Rose's complexion slightly fuchsia.

Rose said, "Counter-offer. After you tell me the story, you make damn sure you come back next week. We'll talk about it then. But no disappearing acts, okay? If that's part of the deal, then I agree to the rest of your terms."

I agreed, "Deal."

She settled back into her high-backed burgundy velvet arm-chair. The emerald around her neck glinted at me, a green light for me to go on.

"Where did I leave you last week? Oh, yeah, out in Washington Square."

A part of me was sitting on Rose's couch telling her a story as the sunlight died. Another part was back Washington Square, three decades ago, feeling the clawing grasp of Veronique's fingers on my arm as she said, "We've got to do something!"

I looked into Veronique's eyes, and I saw the same fear that I felt. This was a real mess. "We could call the cops." I hated the words as they came out of my mouth.

Q just shook her head. She was right. That would make a mockery of everything we were fighting for. I tried again, "Okay, what about trying to talk Ted and the others out of it?"

Q said, "I've spent the past three days trying to do just that. Look, Ted and Terry are not listening to anyone. They've gone completely rogue. Frank is a toady, he'll go along with anything. The dance at Fort Dix is for noncommissioned officers and their dates. All those three can talk about is cutting off the head of the war machine. They're fanatics."

I could see bloody body parts of young college girls peppered with carpet tacks. This was going to turn the whole country against us. And rightfully so. There was no possible justification for this wanton murder. It had to be stopped.

But at what price? I said, "We could steal the bombs."

Q let go of my arm and stepped away. She looked toward the street, scanning up and down. She said, "What good would that

do? They'd just make more bombs. And everyone in the movement would turn on us."

"Okay, goddamn it, I give up. What the hell should we do?"
I was mad, and she was the only one I could attack.

"Richard, I don't know. I've been tearing my hair out. I was
so glad to see you walk in the door this morning. I didn't know
if you'd make it here on time."

"So, I'm here. I don't know what difference that's going to
make."

She turned and looked steadily into my eyes for a very long
minute. Then quietly she said, "We can stop them. I think you
know how."

Then I saw it. To stop the murderer you must become the
murderer. I got dizzy, and my stomach clenched. "Q, you're
crazy. You can't do that."

"You're right. I can't do that. I wouldn't know how. But you
could do that, while I got Paula, Diana, and Kathy out of the
house. But you're right. Maybe that is a crazy idea. Tell me a
better one, please. Or maybe you feel we should just stay unin-
volved. 'How many times must a man turn his head, and pretend
that he just doesn't see?' "

"Don't quote Dylan to me. Just shut up!" She just kept that
constant gaze trained on me.

I walked away from her and sat down on a stone bench, dis-
turbing the pigeon that had been sunning himself there. I bent
over and put my head in my hands. If Bernadette was going to
let them do this, there was no one I could go to for help. They
had the green light from the top. I was not in the upper echelon
of command; I was just the gofer. No one was going to step in.
This was down to Q and me.

I felt a warm hand on my shoulder. Reading my mind, she said, "It's down to us. We can stop this massacre, and put this bomb-making factory out of business. Maybe then our leaders will wake up, and realize that there's a big difference between a powerful symbolic act and a bloodbath."

Not looking up from the cradle of my fingers I said, "And then what? Go to jail for killing our brothers? Or get hunted down by the underground? You better not have any long-range plans, Q."

"I've thought about that. You can make this thing look like an accident. And then we can both disappear. People will either think that we died in the explosion, or that we ran away after it, and quit the movement. Nobody is going to think we did this."

I said, "Excuse me, sweetie, but I don't happen to be independently wealthy. I can't just go underground for the rest of my life."

She squatted down in front of me and gently lifted my head from my hands. Then she took my face in her hands and said, "Richard, I know this seems impossible. But I think in some way we were meant to prevent this tragedy. Last night Paula told me about her father. He's been skimming diamonds off the top of the shipments he brings into this country, and has them all stored in a safe in the upstairs study. If the house goes, he's not going to be able to tell anyone about those rocks. I will get you enough jewels to set yourself up underground, I promise you. But we've got to act right now. They're almost through making the bombs. In a couple of hours they'll be leaving for the dance. If it's going to happen, it's got to go down now!"

I said, "Do whatever you're going to do and get the girls out of the house. In half an hour I'm going back downstairs to help

Ted. At any time after I go down those stairs, the house may blow. Be out of there."

She gave me the lightest of kisses and said, "Thank you, Richard." Then she was gone.

I spent the next half hour getting used to the idea that I was about to commit suicide. I kept rehearsing what I was about to do. I would walk in, chat with Terry upstairs, and then go down. I'd help Ted make some bombs and wait until his back was turned. Then I would connect the battery and detonate a bomb. Then I would die.

This little voice in me was screaming, "No! Run away! Save yourself and screw the rest of this!" I had to put that voice in a thick metal box and padlock the lid closed, or I'd jump in my van and head west. My new mantra was, "There's no one else but me." I kept repeating it over and over, trying to drown out the piercing howl of that little voice.

I thought I had been there just a few minutes, but when I looked at my wristwatch, forty-five had passed. I slowly got to my feet. The sky was a robin's-egg blue. A little blond girl in green shorts giggled as she broke away from her mother and jumped into the fountain. Even the honk of an impatient taxi as it drove by seemed merry. Everything was precious. I stood there savoring each second. Then reluctantly I turned and began walking the three blocks to Eighteen West Eleventh Street.

Terry was reading a newspaper in the living room. Frank was nowhere to be seen. Terry didn't look up as I walked through to the basement stairs. Ted was at the workbench, working on a detonation device.

"Hey, Veronique just told me what you guys are up to. This mission is very cool!"

191

Ted looked up. "She's got a big mouth." He went back to disassembling the clock in front of him.

My heart was beating very fast. I started to sweat. I had to win him over. "Look, count me in. This is the best thing we've done so far. Who the hell cares about a few statues, or an empty police station? You guys are finally going to bring the war home. This is going to wake up the fat, lazy, pro-war, white middle-class. For the first time they'll get a taste of what our Vietnamese brothers and sisters face every day."

He looked up again. This time he smiled at me. "Yeah, Traveler, you got it exactly. And we're going to show those Army cocksuckers that there's another army in this country. One that is a hell of a lot more dangerous than the Viet Cong! There will be no peace anywhere until we break the back of the capitalist dog."

"I want in. What can I do to help?"

He walked away from the table and headed for the shelves of supplies behind us. His back was to me as he spoke. "Actually we're pretty much through here. I need to make three more detonators and wire them up. We've got a lot more sticks of dynamite that need to be wrapped with tape and tacks, but I ran out of tape. If you could go down to the hardware store and get us some more tape and another box of carpet tacks I think we could be through here in about an hour."

Terry and Frank were upstairs. Maybe Q was right. I might live through this. Maybe some force in the universe was working to aid us in stopping this catastrophe. As Ted was speaking, I walked over to the workbench and clicked on the switch that hooked up the battery. Then I headed for the stairs.

"Okay, I'll be right back. Disconnected?"

"Do you think I'm an idiot? Of course. Now, hurry!"

"I'm gone."

Up the stairs, past Terry, still reading, and out the door. I was about half a block down the street when the sidewalk shook. Then the loudest sound I had ever heard swept over me. As I turned around I watched the bricks of the brownstone bulge out. Two more blasts shook the ground. A chunk of masonry went flying past my head. I stood still. If I were meant to die from pieces of that building, it would be a fitting end to my life.

The inside of the building glowed with a red from out of the depths of Hell. Then windows upstairs broke out and flames came out of them. The roofs of cars parked in front of the building were smashed as huge chunks of the façade came raining down on them. The front door opened, and I saw a woman stagger out. It was Kathy! I thought Q was going to get the girls out of there.

A church bell rang the noon hour. I took a step toward the building, when I heard a whooshing sound and flames started pouring out of the building. Glass came shattering down on the street. A cloud of smoke passed over me, smelling of cordite and burned meat. I watched a large piece of concrete break off a cornice and land right next to Kathy. Then a woman I didn't recognize came running up, put her arm around Kathy and walked off with her. I could hear sirens in the distance. Folks were pouring out of their houses to watch. I had to get out of there.

I ducked into a Horn and Hardart's Cafeteria, ran to the men's room, and threw up. I sat on the commode and started to cry. I couldn't stop. I'd just killed at least two people, men I knew really well. And maybe Q, Diana, and Paula, too. Then I got sick again. I stayed in there a long time.

Finally someone was pounding on the door. I got up and walked out into the streets. I started to wander, numb and dead inside.

It's a city of almost eight million people. What are the odds of walking past a jewelry store, looking in, and seeing Veronique? She looked out at the same time, said something to the jeweler, ran out, and threw her arms around me. We both stood there sobbing. Finally she said, "I waited for you in Washington Square, but you didn't come. I thought you died. Oh, God, Richard, what have we done?"

I felt a tiny bit of the load lighten. I was not alone. She shared some of my guilt and horror. I said, "Kathy walked out of the building. I thought you were supposed to get the girls out."

She couldn't talk, she was crying so hard. I felt the dampness of her tears soak through my shirt. Then she said, "No one was there when I went back, except Ted and Terry. Terry told me Frank was sleeping and the girls went out shopping. So I grabbed what I needed and left. I had no idea they came back." Then more tears, from both of us.

I said, "What are we going to do?"

She grasped my arm and dragged me around a corner and into a narrow alley. She opened her purse and grabbed a small manila envelope and said, "Here, take this. We've got to split up and disappear. Go far away. Maybe someday we'll meet again. Richard, I'm so sorry that you had to do that. It's horrible for both of us . . ." Her sobs stopped her, and she just stood there crying.

I looked down at what was in my hand. I could feel something rattle in the envelope. I opened it and dumped the contents into my palm. Sparkling up at me were ten large diamonds, worth a small fortune. I looked back at her. I was hit with the biggest wave of loneliness I'd ever experienced. I felt like Judas with his bag of silver. I wanted to throw everything on the ground. I wanted to take her in my arms. I never wanted to leave her side.

But I didn't act on any of those feelings. Instead I dropped the bright stones back in the envelope and put it in my pocket. I turned and left her standing there weeping. There was nothing more to say.

"There's nothing more to say." There, I'd finally told someone. I looked over at Rose. I don't know what I expected, maybe an expression of horror or disgust. All I could see were her gentle eyes looking back. She played by the rules and said nothing. I kind of wished I hadn't made those rules. A kind word from her would have felt pretty good. But rules were rules. So I got up and walked out into the evening.

CHAPTER THIRTY-THREE

Edward Hightower, aka Strephon Ventnor, sat cross-legged on his meditation bench and closed his eyes. He was silent for ten minutes. Then quietly he spoke his evening prayer.

"Powers of the dark unknown, I am your servant. Use me to awaken the wills, minds, and hearts of those who come to study with me. Awaken my own will and sharpen my intention so that I may serve you better. Teach me and let me love how vast the mystery will always be. In the name of that which cannot be named I dedicate myself to you."

He got up awkwardly, his knees hurting from being bent and immobile. He crossed over to his bed, turned out his light, and tucked himself under the covers. The streetlight on San Pablo didn't bother him. Within ten minutes he was starting to snore.

He slept through the gentle click as his bedroom door opened. He slept through the sound of soft footfalls coming toward his bed.

His eyes opened, startled, when he felt the small cold ring of metal against his temple. He jerked his head around and saw who held the gun. Then came the flash and he heard the loudest sound he'd ever experienced. A terrible smell of burnt flesh. No pain, but blood everywhere.

CHAPTER THIRTY-FOUR

I couldn't remember the last time I'd had a good night's sleep. I was already awake at five when my cell went off. I figured it was a drug dealer with a wrong number, but what the hell, I answered it.

It was Officer James McNally, my one friend on the police force. "Don't say anything. A guy named Hightower got hit last night. A .45 Kimber Team Match II was found near the scene. Five phone calls waking up the owners of snazzy gun shops, and bingo, they got a match on the serial number. The guy who sold it described you pretty well, since you were the only person ever to ask him to remove the red, white, and blue grips and put on a set of checkered walnut ones.

"The arrest warrant just came in. No phone tap authorized yet. They're heading toward your place now, with lots of backup. If you did it you're an idiot. But I don't think you'd be stupid enough to leave your piece behind. Not that gun. You're being set up, dude. This call didn't happen. Bye."

It couldn't be my pistol. It was safely locked up in my Antioch storage locker. They must have the wrong person. All the time I was protesting my innocence to myself, I was in motion. I'd already rehearsed this moment about a thousand times. I grabbed the envelope with the rest of Edward's cash in it, pulled on my sweatpants, a black sweatshirt, and slipped into my Velcro strap sneakers.

I stepped back and looked out the window. Three squad cars, no flashers on, were slowly coming up Hearst. Mac was right on. He must really want that bike shop. Then an unwanted tear seeped out. I had a friend who was willing to risk his job to save my freedom. Damn, I'm not used to that. No time! I grabbed my flight bag, a navy blue backpack with a big UC emblem on the back. It hung by the door, always packed and ready for use. I locked my apartment and ran down the hall for the back steps.

As I was moving, I was thinking, fiercely. Leave by the front door? Run right into the cops. Leave by the side door? Go into an alley that exits right in front of the building, into the arms of the police. Go around back and jump the wall? Get stuck in a row of tiny restaurants that all exit one place, near the front of the apartment house. Climb up to the roof? The roof was two stories higher than any buildings around it. Jump off it and I would end up with broken bones. Three cars, at least six cops. Three cops could button this place up tight while the other three searched inside.

So I can't leave. Where can I wait them out? I don't know anyone in this building well enough to ask them to shelter me from the police. I kept going down, past the side exit, into the basement.

Then I finally figured out what my feet had already known. That weird coal room I found when I went on my knees through the hatch in the laundry room. It was my only hope of refuge.

I dropped under the sorting table and carefully pried open the door. Again the hinges squeaked. I hoped the floor-to-floor search hadn't begun. I crawled through and pulled the hatch closed behind me. It fit snugly. I was in my concrete womb.

Outside was still dark. There was no light coming through the cracks in the cellar door. I sat on the cold floor, keeping my pack on my lap so that it didn't get coal dust all over it. I waited forever.

I had plenty of time to berate myself for that one stupid moment of impulsiveness. Last year, I saw that beautiful gun sitting there in the case, and handed the storeowner $1400 in cash. A written test, a right thumbprint, a demonstration that I knew what I was doing with a gun, a couple of days for the guy to switch the grips, and this gorgeous gun was mine. I didn't think to buy it under another name. I was never going to commit a crime with this beauty. I had other, untraceable guns for that. Fuck!

Finally I heard a man's voice. At first it was unintelligible. Then I heard steps and his voice was louder, ". . . doors all padlocked. I'll check the laundry room." I could hear the squeak of his rubber-soled shoes on the linoleum floor and he walked around the room, only five feet from me.

I could hear the groan of the table as he leaned on it and the click as he pressed down on his walkie-talkie. "The basement's all clear. Let's do a perimeter search, finish the door-to-door, and call it a day. Somehow that son of a bitch got away. We'll get him when he comes back. Watkins out."

A while later I heard more steps coming along the outside wall. Then someone rattled the cellar doors. The brace on my side held them firmly closed. Then nothing.

Shit, I hadn't grabbed my wristwatch. Well I would just have to wait some more. I thought how, if I were a cop, I would stake out Warren's apartment: bugs in my apartment, and two plain-clothes cops, one in the Greek café across the street who could cover the front door and the side alley, and one parked on Hearst to watch the side of the building and the entrance to restaurant alley. Then Mr. Warren Ritter would be boxed in tight.

The clock tower struck eight. I thought about the *Moirae:* the three fates of Greek mythology. There was Clotho: the spinner, creator of the beginnings of your life. Then there was Lachesis: the one who measures. She measured out the length of your life with her rod. Finally came Atropos, with her "abhorred shears." One snip and your life was over. I could feel Atropos breathing down my neck. Had I come to the end of the line? Would I be caught in a shootout? Would my phantom assassin take me out? How much longer did I have to live? I could feel the darkness closing in.

If I was going out, I was not going to go "gentle into that good night." Fuck the fates; I decided to join the furies. They exacted punishment on those whose crimes were not within the range of human justice. Like my lethal adversary out there. From now on my merciless guide would be Tisiphone, the night sister assigned to avenge murder. Fuck with my life? I wanted vengeance.

The clock tower struck nine. Sunlight began to illuminate the cracks in the wooden cellar door and soon I could see inside my tomb. I stood up and took off my sweatshirt, switching my backpack from hand to hand to make sure it didn't get dirty on the floor. The black pants came off next. With one hand I used the clothing to wipe off the ramp that ran up to the cellar door. I spent some time with this, doing my best to make sure that the boards were free from black dust. Then I set my pack down on the ramp and began to unpack it.

First challenge was the board that secured the cellar door. I took my black Swisstool out of the front pocket of my pack and, using the chisel, the crate opener, and the serrated blade, I began prying and cutting away around the large nails that held the bar in place. I took my time, because there was a screech of metal in wood every time I forced the wooden brace up a little more.

It took two hours, but finally I was able to lever off the two-by-four. The hinges looked completely rusted. I didn't have any WD 40 in my kit. But I soaked each hinge with Vaseline Intensive Care Skin Lotion, and hoped for the best.

I used a T-shirt in the pack to wipe off my sweat. Then I opened up the portable makeup kit. It had a battery-powered light on the side of the cosmetic mirror. I set it up on a shelf across from the ramp. With the sun hitting the boards above, my paltry light would not show. I brushed my hair onto the top of my head and fitted on a skullcap, so that no brown hair showed. Then I took out the black wig from its bag in my pack and put it on. Real hair, none of this synthetic shit. For short-hair wigs you couldn't scrimp.

I rinsed off my hands with the bottle of saline solution and put in dark-brown-colored contact lenses. Next, a little eyebrow pencil, and some darker foundation, making sure that it extended below the shirt line, and around the back of my neck. I used to date a girl who worked the Clinique counter. Those white lab jackets were irresistible. We got into some very twisted fantasies involving her products. It was an education in many ways, including the intricacies of makeup. A little more foundation on my hands and wrists, and some powder to matte the finish and I was through.

I put on the navy and gold sweatshirt with the logo of the University of California at Berkeley on the back, and then the blue sweatpants. I put on the clean socks and the running shoes that were in the bag. I fitted the headphones into my ears, and put the MP3 player in the pocket of my windbreaker. I put on the clear wire-rimmed glasses, and took out a thick book titled: *Lectures on Electrical Engineering: Transient Electrical Phenomena. (Vol. 3).* I was ready to boogie.

You may think that no one is going to believe a fifty-five-year-old college student. But they weren't going to see that. They were going to see just another swarthy guy in navy sweats. In the restaurants where I was headed, there were going to be at least three other people dressed almost identically. I blended into the environment.

Next came the most important part. I had to become psychologically invisible. All my aikido meditation practice was needed for this. I concentrated my focus and moved my energy inward. I became contained, centered, calm, and confident. I adopted the mindset of an overextended student, slightly worried about the upcoming exam, absorbed, unaware of his immediate surroundings. In short, I became a nerd.

I stood up and shoved open the cellar doors. I was behind my apartment, in a tiny alleyway. No one else was around.

I ignored the shriek of the hinges, closed the doors behind me, walked up to the retaining wall, and hoisted myself over it into the small outside dining area of a Thai restaurant, as naturally as if that was my usual way of leaving this building.

Without making eye contact with anyone, I started toward the street. I stepped into Top Dog, a gourmet hot dog joint, and ordered a kielbasa. I read my textbook while I waited for the dog to grill. When I got it, I paid, and walked out onto the sidewalk. I don't know where the police were stationed, because I wasn't looking around. I crossed onto the campus eating my hot dog and thinking about electrical engineering. After a few minutes I turned south and began the long walk to Alfredo's Cycles.

CHAPTER THIRTY-FIVE

a l thought it was totally normal that I should show up with different colored eyes and hair. His uncle was a "made man" in the mob, and one of my best private tarot clients. I knew firsthand that this wasn't the strangest thing that had ever happened in his shop.

In a bag in one of Alfredo's lockers I had everything I needed to step into my alternate identity as David Ellbruck. Only trouble was that my Washington driver's license picture didn't look like me with makeup. I wouldn't be able to use the credit cards, but I had plenty of cash. I hoped no cop stopped me. From now on, the speed limit was my friend.

Driving my bike a "safe and sane fifty-five," it took over an hour to get to the storage lockers. I'd always paid for my Antioch storage locker with cash and a phony California ID, so there was no link to Warren Ritter. The owner was usually drunk, passed out in front of the TV in his living room. He'd never checked my ID. I'd just punch in the security code, sign in, and drive on.

As I wheeled up to number 157 I saw trouble. The padlock hung loosely on the hasp. When I rolled up the door I said, "Shit!" The doors on the two big metal lockers inside hung wide open. I could see where the locks were cut out of the doors. There were no guns. My whole collection was missing. So was the small safe that held ten grand in cash reserves." The only thing left were some pistachio nutshells on the floor. Hungry messy, friggin' thieves.

I tried to play detective, searching the place carefully for clues. I collected some of those stupid shells that littered my floor. I picked up a clod of dirt that I hoped I hadn't brought in on my boots. I discovered a tiny piece of gray cloth that got caught on a jagged edge of metal, where they cut the lock out of the door of the inside storage containers. I was doing what I read about in police procedural mysteries.

My sixth sense kicked in, almost too late. Suddenly, I felt very uncomfortable. There was nothing but trouble for me here. I got real itchy, and quickly concluded my investigation by pulling down my locker door, getting on my bike, and booking out of there. Stopping at a light I saw a blue BMW heading for the freeway onramps. I was about to charge through the red light and give chase when a Berkeley patrol car, light flashing but no siren, turned left in front of me, heading toward the storage place. Way out of his territory. I waited until the stoplight changed. By the time I got to the onramps I couldn't tell which one the Z-3 took. I tore off heading south but I didn't find the sports car.

I was being set up at every turn. Well, all those cops were going to find were two empty lockers and a lot of my fingerprints. That sure beat finding me there. I had to discover who was behind all this, and I didn't have much time.

I pulled into a Super 8 motel in the south end of Richmond. No pool, no spa, just a bed, a shower and a twenty-five-inch TV. I watched *Queer Eye for the Straight Guy,* and was again grateful that I didn't own a one-eyed monster. I hooked up the cell phone that I carried in my escape pack to recharge it, and then I crashed.

CHAPTER THIRTY-SIX

You through with your coffee, lady?"

She was done with Denny's. She was tired of fluorescent lights, shiny plastic-coated menus, and Muzak. Ed's Chevron Truck Stop Café, south of Union City had just what she was looking for, a bunch of shit-kicking patrons, no music, the smell of old, hot grease, and a trucker's steak and eggs breakfast available anytime.

She picked the last shred of rare steak out of her teeth and was settling back into her booth to write, when Ed came by to harass her. She figured he wanted to get rid of her. He was a thin, nervous guy, hairy except for the top of his head. Everywhere else he sprouted curly black threads. She looked at him, and noticed the contracted pupils. *I'd be on speed, too, if I had his job,* she thought.

But Ed was there to serve her. She liked being served. She hated to cook for herself. It felt good to be waited on. "I'll have a slice of pumpkin pie with whipped cream."

That would keep him off her back for a while. She took out her journal and began to write.

It's like the song says, "You might serve the devil, or you might serve the Lord, but we all gotta serve someone." It's time for Mr. Warren Ritter to serve me.

The shells on his storage locker floor, and the anonymous tip sending the cops out to Antioch were particularly inspired. It was close. I only wish they could have caught the son of a bitch there.

But actually that's not good thinking. I take that back. I want him on the loose. Let the Border collies chase him around California for another forty-eight hours. Then I won't care.

First thing on the itinerary: a quick flight to the Caymans. Again the she-wolf will outfox the hounds. It's so easy to make money disappear. All I have to do is walk into that bank and withdraw the whole thing in cash. Pounds, I think, that will be lighter. Then I carry them down the street and into another bank. Deposit it. No electronic trail. No connection between the two transactions. I'm scot-free.

I have one last thread to clip. I've got to head for Mexico City, and have one hell of a good time with Anthony. When I'm tired of him, I will need to find a very clever way to administer his own poison back to him. Poetic justice, I think.

Then off on my world tour. Retribution accomplished. Life is sweet.

She closed her book, and leaned back to savor her last bite of pie. She looked at the truckers and hookers around her. She knew that soon she would visit the Riviera and play *Chemin de Fer* with princes. But these folks, scarfing down their steaks, would always be the closest thing she felt to her kind of people.

CHAPTER THIRTY-SEVEN

I slept until noon. That's very unlike me. It's just that every time I opened my eyes, I couldn't find a good reason to get out of bed. So I closed them and hoped that everything would just go away and leave me alone. Finally I realized that reality wasn't going away anytime soon, so I better get up and face it.

I showered, turned on the TV, and reapplied my disguise while savoring the Home Shopping Network. Then I picked up my cell and spoke Mac's name into it. Soon I heard, "Officer McNally here."

"Yo, biker boy, this is your moneybags. What's happening?"

"Who? Oh. Call me back in ten minutes."

"Gotcha."

I thought seriously about buying that diamond-and-sapphire pendant on the shopper's channel. I could send it to my daughter from prison. Ten minutes was up.

I kept up the phony street jive from the seventies. "What's the hap's, dude?"

He was nonchalant. "Oh, nothing much. You know we had the funniest case in the station house last night. The head of a satanic cult got popped. The perp dropped his gun near the scene of the crime, a gun so specialized that it only took about an hour to trace it.

"But wait, there's more. An anonymous tip led us to his storage locker, which he had emptied out, after breaking all the locks inside and outside of it. The only thing he left were some shells from a poisonous nut, the same poison that was used to kill the CFO of that devil church just last week. What a fucking idiot this guy is."

I said, "It shouldn't take too long to catch him."

"Nope, not if he's dumb enough to hang around here. There was one other dim-witted move that the perp made. He shot the victim in the head, and walked off. Must have seen too many cop shows where the crooks all roll over cooperatively and die in a second. The bullet went right through the skull and didn't hit anything critical. The victim crawled over toward his phone and tried to make a call. He pulled the phone to the floor, but must have known that he wasn't gong to last long enough to get to it. He used his own blood to scribble something and to paint some symbols on the floor before he bled to death. We can't decipher the writing. Starts with an M or a W or something. We figure he was trying to summon up some demonic support. I guess it didn't work."

"Oh yeah. Interesting story. What were the symbols?"

"A snake climbing a pole and two squares. Mean anything to you?"

"A conversation between two Republican doctors?"

"Maybe. So what are you up to?"

I had no intention of telling him that. "Look, dude, I gotta run. You hang loose and maybe I'll check in tomorrow. Is that cool?"

"Sure, cool as ice. You be careful out there."

He meant it. It meant a lot to me right now that someone cared. He didn't have to keep taking these risks. He was a true friend. Of course I didn't tell him that. Instead I said, "Later" and snapped my phone shut.

I made a sketch of the symbols. I didn't think they were about demonology. Edward was trying to tell someone who shot him. And, considering how much he distrusted the police, I doubted that he was writing to them. No, it was to either Veronique or to me. I wondered if Edward could write Japanese. I moved the paper around, flipped it upside down. I needed to know where the symbols were in relationship to each other.

Then I saw something. I hit redial. "Dude, was the head of the snake facing right or left?"

"Um, let me think. Facing to toward the body, which would be to the right. Why?"

"Later."

I had to get inside that church.

I couldn't get inside that church. It was a fucking crime scene. Bright yellow tape on the doors announcing to pedestrians, CRIME SCENE—DO NOT CROSS" A squad car was parked in front. But there was a typed note on the door, so I risked walking up and reading it. I really hoped this disguise worked.

NO SERVICES THIS WEEK it read. Not much of a tribute to Edward. For this I risked my neck? I walked back to my bike and rode off, watching carefully for any tail. It looked like I was clear. I pulled into the parking lot of a deserted clothing store and called Max Valdez.

"Valdez Security, how may I help you?"

"Hi, Isabel. Is Max in?"

"He's in all right, and pretty mad at you, Warren."

Max cut in, "Off the line, Isabel. I thought I told you no trouble. Then I see an APB out for you. What's going on?"

Isabel was right, he was mad. I didn't want him to hang up on me. "First of all, Max, this isn't like last time. No cops are going to show up to search your offices. There is nothing connecting me to you. I'm calling from a cell phone that Heather pays for. Before, when I called, I was at a booth. I never took any notes on our conversations. So you are in the clear, I promise."

"Good. I better be. Now what's going on?"

"Someone's trying to nail this murder on me, and a whole string of other murders. I need your help."

Max said, "I try not to work with people who are the target of a statewide manhunt." I got a sinking, all-alone feeling. But then he said, "What do you want?"

"I've got to get into that church."

"Why?"

I didn't want to tell Max about my flimsy conjectures. I'd decided that Edward's symbols weren't about a snake and pole at all. I figured he'd been trying to sketch a dollar sign. But if I was wrong I'd look like an utter fool.

But I couldn't lie to Max, not at this point. I decided to shade the truth a little. "Edward told me before he died to follow the money. I've got to get into their financial records and see who is benefitting from all these deaths."

Max said, "Well, you're out of luck. His apartment was in the church building and the cops are not going to let you or any of my people go waltzing in. But, Warren, as you know, that's not the only way to get the information you want."

Oh, oh. "Sally and I are not talking right now."

"Well you better get talking or she's going to have to visit you in San Quentin."

I didn't need this. I wanted Max and Heather just to bug out and leave me alone. I could handle Sally. I'd just wait until she contacted me. And die of old age.

"Are you there, Warren?"

"Yeah, yeah, I'm here. Just thinking about what you said. But I don't even know what bank the church uses."

He said, "Churches are nonprofit corporations in California. It would only take me half an hour to track their corporate ID number and trace it to a bank. Here's what I'd do if I wanted to make that trace. I'd call Sally and ask her to start hacking."

"Would you?"

"Knock it off, Warren. Make the fucking call. Talk to you later."

I deserved to get hung up on. I was a chicken. But I didn't want to be a chicken in the slammer. This was not how I wanted to reconnect. Muttering about beggars and choosers I dialed her number.

She answered. "I thought I told you not to call." She always knew who was calling her.

"If there was any way on God's green earth that I could avoid bothering you right now, I would take it. But I can't. I need your expertise, even if you hate my guts. I'm getting framed for murder again. Twice in one year, that must be a record. Somebody shot my client, set me up, and I'm running around in a wig."

"So?"

"Look, I could just drive away from all this. You should know how tempting that is to me. But I won't, and you're the reason why. Even though you think I'm the sexist asshole of the year, I still believe that you'll come back. So I'm risking getting arrested and tried for murder because I love you. Could you give me something besides a 'So'?"

"What do you want, Warren?"

So, this was Sally's version of warming up. I'd never seen her this angry before. She must really feel vulnerable. I'd need to keep this on a professional level so she didn't bolt. "Edward wanted me to follow the money. I think that meant for me to find out who in his church was profiting from these murders. I need you to hack the church's bank account and tell me if you see anything suspicious."

"You wouldn't happen to know their bank or have an account number by any chance?"

"No, unfortunately. The church is called the Fellowship of the Arising Night and it's incorporated in California. That's all I know."

"When do you need this, Warren?" I could hear the clicking of her keyboard in the background.

"Well, the manhunt has gone statewide according to Max, so anytime soon would be good."

She sighed. "Call me back in half an hour."

That was an opening if I ever heard one. I was smiling. "Thank you so much. Sally. I owe—"

She interrupted me. "Just call back in half an hour. Drop

the sweet stuff." *Click.* She wasn't the easiest person in the world to love.

"Hi, Warren. Another hour." *Click.*

"Forty-five minutes. I'm almost through Bank of America's ice."

Boy was I overusing my redial button today.

Sally answered, "I got in. Hightower sure pointed you in the right direction. A month ago a trustee from the estate of Richard Steed, the unfortunate victim of a hit-and-run accident, delivered a check for one million dollars to the church. Three days ago Edward Hightower made a wire transfer to the Bank of Butterfield International in the Cayman Islands for $865,000. This is a very modern bank. They even have a twenty-four-hour bank-by-phone number. I have the account number it was deposited to, but without the password I couldn't get any further. Besides, who knows, it may have been transferred out of there and into five different accounts by now. Find out who owns that account and I bet you'll find our killer."

"Give me the telephone number of the bank and the account number anyway. Sally, you're a queen."

She gave me the numbers and then said, "I'm still not ready to talk with you, Warren. But good luck." *Click.*

I called the Pizza Hut in El Cerrito and asked them to deliver a medium mushroom, sausage, and onion pan pizza. While I waited for dinner I briefly contemplated shooting myself, but then I remembered that I didn't have any guns. Not knowing what else I could do, I wolfed down my pizza, doubled my anti-depressive medication, and headed for Hayward. If I couldn't get into the Den of Satan, I sure as hell was going to try to get in the House of the Lord.

CHAPTER THIRTY-EIGHT

No lights were on inside the concrete block structure, but the front was flooded with a spotlight.
The fog was back but not thick enough to ob-
scure the two suits who were smoking cigarettes
as they lounged by the front door. I drove around
the block to a spot I estimated should be right behind the
church. The last time I'd done a B & E, Max's operatives had
unlocked the door for me. After that escapade Max had been
more than willing to teach me how to open some locked doors
for myself. I had a carefully carved plastic card in my wallet. If
the door had a deadbolt I'd be screwed. Otherwise I had a
chance.

The house I parked my bike in front of was dark. Two news-
papers lay on the front porch. Nobody home. Thank you, Jesus.
I walked around the house and easily climbed over the chain-
link fence in the back. I was in the middle of a playground. The
rear side of the church was not lit but a dim bulb glowed over
the back door. I sat down behind the slide structure and waited.

One goon made a circuit every thirty minutes, regularly as clockwork.

After he turned the corner the third time I got up and scampered up to the back door. It had a door lock and a separate deadbolt. Shit! I jammed my tool in the space between the door frame and the door lock for the fun of it. I eased the latch bolt back and pulled on the knob. The door opened. Someone forgot to double lock it. Truly, goodness and mercy shall follow me all the days of my life. I slipped in, shut the door behind me, and made sure the door was still locked from the outside.

Now we'll find out about motion detectors or infrared beams. Well, I'd been beaten up already by these guys. What's a few more bruises? I walked down the hall, opening and closing doors. Then I saw the one marked REV. MORRISON. That was my suspect. Bingo. It was locked, but that lock was a piece of gateau. Again, I shut the door behind me.

Lots of light came flooding in from the spotlight shining outside the window, almost as bright as if the light were on inside. I looked around. Not much to look at: bookshelf, desk, and file cabinet. I went over to the file cabinet. On top of it was a book, with a photograph stuck into the middle of the book.

I almost ignored it. Then the picture on the cover registered: a crowd of demonstrators. One guy had a helmet on. Another, next to him, had shades. It was JJ and Terry from the New York collective. I held the book up to the light to see better: *Bringing the War Home: The Weather Underground, the Red Army Faction, and Revolutionary Violence in the Sixties and Seventies.* Yikes.

Then I opened to the page where the photo was. Someone in her congregation was a good photographer. The photo was a black-and-white eight-by-ten taken just outside of Hightower's satan temple. It was a telephoto shot of Veronique and Strephon/ Edward walking together, arm in arm. I turned it over. On the back someone had written "6/14–Edward Hightower and his sister, Veronique Hightower."

Then I looked at the book. One half of the page had a close-up of a woman in a helmet. The caption read "Anonymous Weatherwoman during the Days of Rage." You could see the resemblance between the women in those two photos clearly. Above the picture, in bold magic marker, someone had correctly identified it, "Veronique Hightower!"

I checked the front. The book had come out in January. This was an honest-to-god clue! I liked this. I wanted to find some more!

I opened her file cabinet, but everything looked church-related. I went over to her desk and started slowly going through her drawers. Nothing of interest in the side drawers, but the wide one yielded what I was looking for. I lifted out the plastic tray holding paperclips, tacks, tape, and pens. Under it was a manila folder. I opened it.

A color photo dropped onto the desk. It showed a long-haired guy in his twenties. In the corner was a handwritten note, "Love you, sis!" I knew that face much too well. It was Frank Walters, the guy who was asleep upstairs in the townhouse when the bomb that I booby-trapped went off. Shit. Her brother.

I put everything back very carefully. I checked my watch. It was between the half-hour circuits. I opened the office door and locked it behind me. I padded to the back door and carefully opened it a slit to look around. All quiet on the playground front. I shut the door and made sure it too was locked.

I was halfway up the fence when the beam of the flashlight hit me. "Stop right there or I'll shoot!" I didn't. Instead I flew over that fence as I heard the heavy footfalls of someone running toward me. *Don't shoot, don't shoot, don't shoot.*

When you buy a $36,000 bike you expect it to start instantly every time. And mine did. I was around the block and into the mist before Sluggo ever got over the fence. Hey, this was fun! A new kind of antidepressant. Hard to get patented though.

CHAPTER THIRTY-NINE

I woke up feeling great, except for the voice that I thought I heard. It was just as I woke up, so I wasn't sure if it was a dream or what. But it was the voice of Ted Allen, the guy in glasses who cooks for *Queer Eye*. "Hey, big boy, they're going to grab you today!" I looked at the TV but it was definitely off. I hate those hallucinations. One of the more annoying aspects of my mental condition. Oh, well.

Otherwise, I was on top of the world. Finally that pesky depression had lifted. I remembered that I had endured some wild, grotesque dreams last night, but their impact faded quickly. All I could remember was something about firing cap pistols at bats on the firing range. Forget the dreams. Today was a day for action.

I decided that I didn't need to worry about stupid disguises anymore. No one was going to recognize me. It's all in the mind-set. I was a Ninja warrior, unseen until I strike. After all, hadn't I slipped out from right underneath their noses? Today, I was invincible.

I thought about bopping over to Sally's. She should be over whatever was eating her. Maybe we could go out to lunch. We could invite Rose and make it a threesome. I thought about what it would be like in bed with those two.

No, that wouldn't work. Sally would just be a downer. Besides, I had to start to plan the rest of my life. Berkeley was getting too claustrophobic. Someone was always accusing me of murdering someone. That was getting really old.

Then it came in a flash. I should go live with my daughter. She seemed to like me, kind of. Anyway, she would grow to like me. I'm a very likeable guy when I'm not depressed. And I could be the live-in gramps. Take care of the kid, do some cooking and housework. Watch my grandson grow up. Wouldn't that be amazing! I had to tell her my idea.

But not on the phone. She'd want to see me in person. Besides, it was time I met her husband, not to mention little Justin. I wolfed down the rest of the cold pizza (one of my favorite breakfasts), jumped on my bike, and headed south.

I was Mr. Invisible. I flew down the roads, and every policeman looked the other way. I could control their thoughts, and make them ignore the road warrior who just flashed past.

I flew over the hill and into Santa Cruz in record time. I was cruising around Walk Circle, a tight circular road near the center of a series of concentric streets, when I saw the cop car in front of number forty-two, the white clapboard cottage that was the home of my daughter.

They were onto me. They had figured out exactly who I was, and had traced her down. They were in there right now, probably setting up a trap for me. If I had come a half-hour later, I would have ended up in prison. Was she wearing a wire when she saw me at the boardwalk? Had this whole thing been a sting operation to reel me in?

I drove past and continued around the bend, until I was almost out of sight of their front porch. I scanned the area for other police cruisers, but the place looked clear. I'd outfoxed them again.

The front door opened and a guy in uniform started to walk down the steps. Then he turned and said something else to the person inside. My daughter came to the front door and spoke a few words. Then she walked over to the steps, bent over, and kissed the cop. He turned and got into his squad car.

That was her husband. Orrin was a pig. That was why my sister sounded so amused when she spoke about him.

Sometimes you don't wake up from a manic jag for a while. You just rush around, having grand plans, thinking vast eternal thoughts, making royal messes on full speed for days. But occasionally you can get such a shock that it bounces you right out.

What was I thinking? I nearly made a fool of myself waltzing into my daughter's house unannounced to set up housekeeping. A statewide APB was out on me. Sooner or later her husband would connect the dots, and take me in. And then she could tell little Justin all about Grandpa in the slammer.

Jesus, I was on a manic spike. Thank God I hadn't done anything disastrous. Good news, I carry emergency meds on my bike. The bad news was that no medication can stop a manic run immediately. But I found a combination that works pretty fast for me, assuming it doesn't kill me or give me permanent neurological damage. I was already on my antidepressant, even

227

though I had missed this morning's dose. I dumped one of those in my hand. Then I opened the other bottle.

I hated this drug. Someday it was going to leave me shaking like I had palsy. I had used it three times. It wasn't an instant cure, by any means. But it was faster than lithium. And I needed help right now! I shook out two capsules of Seroquel, and swallowed the pills dry.

Grapefruit would make me sick from now on. No great loss there. Also there was the old warning, "Do not operate vehicles if drowsy." Well, I wasn't going to walk my bike back home, so I'd just have to risk it. I headed back to my crummy Super 8 motel room at a very conservative speed.

CHAPTER FORTY

I had a lot to think about on that ride north. Mostly about how I sucked as a detective. I didn't have much to go on, except a link between the reverend and Veronique, and Edward's scrawled symbols. I might as well stir the hornet's nest.

Hayward was on my way home, so I headed for Rev. Morrison's church. On the way I kicked myself again for alienating Sally. She could have found out exactly what the connection was between the good reverend and Frank Walters. Plus she could tell me where Morrison got her money. Maybe I should call her again. No, I already pissed her off doing that last time.

I should have had Max check Morrison out better. I was such a klutz at all this. Now, I had to walk in blind.

I was in luck. There was a cleaning party putting in some shrubbery in front of the building. It was a building so ugly that it needed a lot of shrubbery. I wished they would consult the thirteenth fairy who did the hedge work around Sleeping Beauty's castle.

When I asked for Morrison, an emaciated, elongated woman took my hand and led me into the building. This congregation was much too touchy-feely for me. She walked over to a door I already knew well. One of the gray suits was posted in front of the door. Once depositing me in front of him, my guide faded away.

The guard said, "Greetings and blessings. May I tell the reverend who you are?"

"My name's Warren Ritter."

The guard squinted and looked at me. "I'll have to check you for weapons, Mr. Ritter."

My fame preceded me. I let him pat me down expertly. He left me for a moment and then came back. "Go in, Mr. Ritter."

I walked into the office alone.

Rev. Morrison was writing at her desk, and did not look up immediately. I heard the door click shut behind me. That made me uneasy. I don't know which was worse, having a goon behind me or being trapped in an enclosed space with a five-foot-three, two-legged tiger.

She finally looked at me. When her eyes met mine I could smell the ozone from the energy link. I started to sweat, and again there was this urge to fall to my knees and serve this goddess for the rest of my life. She had a plain, lean face: nose a little hawk-like, lips thin, cheekbone cut deep and missing any superfluous padding. But those eyes. I can't even tell you what color they were. She just pinned you and held you with them.

I realized that my mania had tricked me again. It takes a while for those meds to kick in. Here I was over my head in a situation completely out of my control. And the last time I had had any contact with this church I had ended up with a concussion. God help me this time.

She finally said, "I thought I had discouraged you from interfering with me."

"I'm not so easily diverted."

"I see that. How may I help you today, Mr. Ritter?"

I'd speak my lines the way I'd rehearsed them on the ride up. "I am here about the murder of Edward Hightower."

She let a miniscule grin touch the corners of her mouth. "Yes, sometimes the Lord does *not* move in mysterious ways. Sometimes he just strikes down the wicked. What about Edward Hightower: Priest of the Devil?"

"I know about the money."

She cocked her head. "What are you talking about?"

"The Cayman Islands. And I know about the squares."

Hey, they were the only clues I had; I was going to trot out the whole monkey show.

"You are a strange man, Mr. Ritter. I have no idea what you are talking about. Now why are you here?"

Hardball time. "Look, I've talked with your mother. She tells me you are more than capable of murder. In fact she believes that you may have killed before. Now, what is your connection with Edward Hightower and the eight hundred grand?"

She was silent.

"And your thugs don't scare me any!" (A flat-out lie).

She pushed her chair back from her desk. I took a step backward.

She said through thin lips, "My mother. You spoke to my mother on Tuesday. And now you have solved your little crime. You are a very stupid man.

"Did Mommie dearest tell you, by any chance, that my father repeatedly raped me while she watched? Did she tell you, by any chance, that she has been incarcerated in mental hospitals three times for paranoid delusions? And did she mention that the reason I divorced my husband was because he had an affair with *her?* I bet she left some of those juicy tidbits out of the conversation."

It was all or nothing. "And I know about your brother Frank."

That stopped her. She was still for a moment. "So you were the motorcycle marauder last night. I guess you found his picture."

Then, in a much softer tone she said, "He's my half-brother. Or was. A real good guy. I still miss him. What do you know about him?"

"I know you hate Veronique because she was a Weatherman, just like he was." I was really fishing.

The softness disappeared. "Yes, she was. I do hate Veronique. I do hate that unholy movement that took Frank's life. And I do hate Hightower. Hate makes me strong.

"You probably think Christians shouldn't hate. But I am a weapon of the Lord. The Bible says, 'These six things doth the Lord hate: yea, seven are an abomination unto him: haughty eyes, a lying tongue, hands that shed innocent blood, a heart that devises wicked schemes, feet that are swift in running to mischief, a false witness who utters lies, and he who sows discord among brothers.' Both of the Hightower demons were all these things. I wrote that fiend and warned him about the Lord's retribution. However I'm no murderer."

In a tight, very controlled voice she went on, "Mr. Ritter, for your information, I was leading an all-night prayer vigil Wednesday night and Thursday morning for our troops overseas.

I have a church full of witnesses. Isn't Wednesday night the time that the papers say the Hightower monster was assassinated?

"I was grateful that someone else took on the responsibility of ridding the world of another fiend. But I assure you, I follow the commandments, and I live in Christ's love. Sometimes the Lord doesn't mind if a few heads get cracked, but I would never take another's life, not even Edward Hightower's. Not even yours."

Maybe she was lying. But I wasn't going to get any further with her. I did the only thing I could think of to do. I said, "Thank you for your time, Reverend. I must be mistaken. Have a good day."

I turned and walked out as she said to my back, "Lord have mercy on your soul, Mr. Ritter. And, unless you seek salvation, stay out of my church!"

CHAPTER FORTY-ONE

J ust because you realize you are in a manic state doesn't mean it goes away. You keep making impulsive decisions. It's just that, with a little awareness of your insanity, you tone down some of the more crackpot ones: like a *ménage à trois* with Rose and Sally. Instead you choose the ones that are a little less crackpot. Therefore, I headed out to Heavenly Deliveries the El Cerrito Angels-R-Us store.

Just my rotten luck, there was Grace all by herself, neatening up a display of greeting cards. She turned and smiled at me. "Oh, I was just thinking of you. We got a new deck in the other day that I think you will love. It's called Tarot of the Dark Sun, and it's quite amazing."

This was the day for graceless blundering. "Hello, Grace, or should I say Gloria?"

The smile flattened, the eyes turned glacial. She walked over to the front display, and picked up a sign that had a cherub heading for an outhouse and script that said, I'LL BE RIGHT BACK! I stepped out of the way as she hung it on the front door, and then pushed in the lock on the knob. Then she turned and faced me. "What do you want?"

"I'm here about the murder of Edward Hightower."

She turned pale, looking more shocked than she had when I had called her Gloria. "What about it?"

"Where were you Wednesday night?"

"Home alone, just like every other night. What's the big idea—"

"I know about the money." It was a poor script, but it was the only one I had. This time it had quite an impact.

"God, don't tell me he told somebody about me. He swore he'd keep it a secret!"

Did I hit the jackpot? I tried to imagine those two as secret lovers. She was not Edward's type, whatever that might be. I kept poking. "He gave you money regularly."

"Thank God he did. You don't see this store jammed with customers, do you? He's the only reason I'm still in business. He thought it was amusing, considering the contrasts in our clientele."

Now that sounded like Edward. But why would she kill him? I asked, "Did you love him?"

The tough-broad mask started to melt, and I saw a vulnerable little girl look out of those eyes. She started to cry. "Sometimes I hated him. I mean where was he when I was getting tossed from one hell hole foster home to another? And sometimes I felt like he was the only person in my life that just gave anything to me without wanting something in return.

"I hated that he was a cult leader. I even tried to scare him so bad he would leave it. It didn't work. But he never talked about it with me. He never tried to convert me and he always respected my beliefs."

Then the tears really started to flow. She couldn't talk for a minute. "I don't know if I loved him. I've only known him for seven years. I never let myself think about my father until he finally tracked me down. He did more than track me down. He gave me a whole new identity. He helped me pull myself out of the hole I was digging, which was getting pretty deep. So, yes, I guess I loved him."

Oh. I decided to skip the questions about the Cayman Islands and the squares. She looked pretty upset. I had to find out one thing that was still bothering me. "Look, your father hired me to look into some murders of church members. I traced those e-mails you sent him back to you. I thought you might be a suspect. That's why I had you tailed—"

"Oh, thank God! That was you. I knew someone was watching me. I could feel it. After I read about that lady who was burned up out in the woods, I thought someone was getting ready to kill me next. I must have looked pretty crazy slipping out side doors and going through bathroom windows."

I said, "I'm glad that part is over now. And I'm sorry for any worry I may have caused you. I'm very sorry about your loss. I assure you that I will keep all this confidential.

"I think you are about to come into a pretty substantial legacy. My advice would be to stop trying to put on the brave, stoic face. Close up the shop for a week or so. Let yourself grieve. Also, I'm writing down the phone number of an absolutely wonderful therapist. Her name is Rose Janeworth. Call

237

her right after I leave. You deserve some support right now."

She said something that I couldn't quite make out through the Kleenexes. I was almost out of the door when she stopped me.

"Warren, remember that avenging angel with the flaming sword?"

"Yes, Barakiel, right?"

She stopped crying and looked right into me. "Be my Barakiel. Find the son of a bitch who killed my father."

It was a good performance. Maybe even genuine. But I couldn't help thinking that most murders happen between family members. She loved and hated her father. Interesting. She wasn't out of the running, yet.

CHAPTER FORTY-TWO

Well, I hadn't gotten myself killed yet today, so I thought I'd try that next. I headed over to Miko's. She was my number-one suspect, after all.

Mitsue met me at the door. Her eyes were red and her clothes mussed. She glared at me suspiciously. "Are you FBI?"

I laughed. "I'd sooner be dead. I hate the FBI. Why?"

She managed a tiny smile. "Okay, good. What do you want?"

"I wanted to talk to Miko."

She tilted her head and her brows wrinkled. "You haven't heard?"

"No, heard what?"

She said, "Stay there," and walked up the stairs. She came back with a wrinkled *San Francisco Chronicle* from last Thursday. I'd been on the run since then, and hadn't even glanced at a paper. The headline read:

FBI DEPORTS JAPANESE MOB

Twenty-three suspected associates of the Japanese Yakusa clans and their family members were rounded up Wednesday afternoon and deported to Japan. FBI Director Howard Strabner made this statement: "Recent investigations have uncovered a link between suspected arms sales to Al Qaeda and the Japanese underground. As a matter of homeland security, suspected members of the Japanese mob have been summarily deported without hearings."

The ACLU immediately filed a writ . . .

I stopped reading and looked up at the roommate. "Miko?"
She nodded.
"When did they grab her?"
"They came by Wednesday morning and took her. What did Miko ever do? I'm afraid. When are they going to come to get me?"

I handed her back her paper. "We all need to start worrying about that. Thanks for your help. I'm sorry about your friend."

I still couldn't cross her off my list. Miko didn't sneak out of FBI custody to shoot Edward Hightower. But she still could have hired the person who did the job.

I drove back to my seedy motel room, took some more meds, and flopped down on the bed. I still had too many suspects and not enough evidence. I thought back over everything I had learned. The Reverend Morrison had a great alibi, but one of her thugs might have finished off Hightower. Ditto for Miko.

Grace Westin, my angel lady, had no alibi, but very convincing tears. I was nowhere.

I decided to focus on something more immediately crucial: pizza again or Chinese tonight? I started looking around for the phone book when I noticed on the nightstand the sheet of paper that had Edward's last symbolic message.

I picked it up. Money and squares. M or W. It could be any of my suspects. I tossed my drawing on the bed and finally made up my mind. Tonight: Hawaiian deep-dish. I glanced at the paper again, and then I saw it.

They weren't squares at all. I got very cold. Relay after relay clicked in my mind. Oh, my God. That can't be true. Not that! Just then my cell rang.

It was Max. "I just heard something very interesting. I thought, 'Hey, my friend would like to hear this amusing story.' So I'm calling you."

I could hear the sounds of people, Mariachi music, and glasses clinking behind him. This was no social call. "I'm listening."

"One of my compadres does a lot of freelance work. I was having a drink with him a couple of minutes ago and he told me about a loco white lady, who spoke perfect Spanish. She had a funny trick she wanted to play on this guy she was dating. So she gave my friend a . . . what's the word for that little revolver judges use to start a race?"

I started to see where this was going. "A blank gun."

"Yes. She gave him a blank gun, money to rent a car, and set him up outside a Berkeley restaurant. When she came walking along with her date, he shot at them. She fell down and he drove off. Ha ha, pretty strange. What a loco lady, right?" He did not sound amused.

241

"Thanks, Max. I just got to that page from a different route. I've got to go. I appreciate you getting to me with this. It's the icing on the cake."

"Need any backup?"

"No, this one I've got to do all by myself. Thanks, anyway. Enjoy your evening."

CHAPTER FORTY-THREE

She was through packing. Time for one final entry before heading to the airport. She wondered, again, about what she would do with this journal. Keep it close to her chest until after Mexico, that's for sure. Maybe someday she'd find a ghost writer to bring her story to the world. She'd title it "Retribution: Diary of a Lethal She-wolf." She started writing.

Retribution. It is one of my favorite words. It doesn't mean what most people think it means. It's "a reward, recompense, or requital." In my case, a reward for all my hard work.

Up until now my life has been scratching from con to con. The money from the diamonds I got in the seventies didn't last very long. Then it was just one slippery slide after another. Each setup promising enough money to really be able to relax. And each one falling so short.

Then I came to Berkeley and found my brother's little cult. Finally, ongoing financial security. It's too bad I had to eliminate so many obstacles. But no omelet without a few broken shells. My brother was an asshole anyway. He got what he deserved.

God, that initial job was a bitch. You'd think running somebody over would be easy. But first I had to find an old junker that already had a crumpled front fender. That took two days. Then there's the hotwiring of the car. Thank God for the Internet! Detailed instructions complete with illustrations.

Then the most boring part: tailing the mark. Nothing happens for hours. I almost pissed in my pants when that cruiser stopped to see if I was all right. All they had to do was check my tags and I would have been completely busted for grand theft auto. Sometimes a smile and a little cleavage is a lifesaver.

The next day, when I had a good clear run at him, some friggin' bystander wouldn't move on. But I guess I was lucky. My man was an early morning jogger with a very regular schedule. On the third day I nailed him. Then I ran the car through a car wash and parked it where I stole it. No one probably knew it was missing.

Number two was just a simple push. But damn if there wasn't a meddling witness every time the right opportunity came along. My victim started to get suspicious at seeing the same person almost every time he went walking his dog.

I've already written about poor Ella. It's too soon to think about my brother.

The only people who'd wonder why I did it would be sheep. Any wolf would see the brilliance in my work. Soldiers kill to follow orders. It's their job. Cops kill to do their job. I did my job, and now comes my retribution.

CHAPTER FORTY-FOUR

Her door was unlocked, so I walked right in. She was sitting at a desk writing. A large suitcase filled with clothes sat next to her. She looked up and smiled and said, "Warren, how kind of you to come over and be with me."

I had already rehearsed these lines before. "I'm here to talk about the murder of your brother."

She got up out of her chair. "Do you have a clue as to who did it?"

"I know about the money."

She moved around the table toward me. "What are you talking about?"

"The Cayman Island transfer."

No, she wasn't moving toward me. She reached into her suitcase and picked up a very lethal-looking Beretta Tomcat. I knew it had hollow-point .32s in it and one shot would stop me forever. I also knew it had a small scratch on the right side of its very short barrel. I knew all this, because it was one of my guns.

I diverted from my script. "What did you do with the rest of my stuff?"

"Tossed everything else in the bay. This little piece was so cute I thought I'd hold on to it for a while. In case I needed it. I kept the money. Thanks for the donation. You covered the cost of the PI I hired to tail you this week. He told me all about your locker. By the way, your security is laughable."

I was fucked. "You killed what, four people. Why?"

"Because I could, little black sheep."

Black sheep? Was she a little crazy? Keep her talking. "Tell me about the Cayman Island transfer."

"It took a month of kissing up to Ella, that fat pig, before I could weasel the password to the church's bank account from her. I finally found it on the last page of her diary, written backward. Real clever code! God, she stank. I had to take a long shower after every date to get her smell off me. I was glad to see her barbecued."

No, Max, I don't need backup. What would I need backup for? I wasn't going to live long enough for my meds to take effect. I couldn't do anything else so I asked another question. "Were you the one who transferred the money?"

"Yes, Warren-Richard; you're so clever. I transferred the money. Tonight I am flying down there. Monday morning, early, I am taking my money out of Butterfield International Limited and putting it somewhere else."

"And you killed your brother." I was so brilliant.

"Among others. Once I found out that Steed wrote a will leaving a ton of money to the church, my plans were set. But dear old Strephon-Edward never knew. He always suspected that I was a different breed, but he had no idea how different.

He figured he could handle me. He only knew how wrong he was, when he saw me pointing your gun at his head. What a bozo."

"And what are your plans for me?"

"Warren, I want you very much alive. I would have terminated you when you came through that door otherwise. I want you unarmed and on the run, not dead. At first I thought I wanted the pigs to catch you at your storage locker. That's why I bribed the clerk to tell me when you came there to check out my little robbery. I tipped the cops, but you got away.

"Then I realized that it was better for you to be on the run. I want them chasing you for a few more days, while I disappear. As long as the cops are after you, they'll leave me alone. All I need is forty-eight hours and Veronique Hightower is no more. So, unless you try to be a stupid hero, you can leave with my blessing. Do you need any extra cash? I'd be more than willing to help you get far away from here."

Oddly enough, I didn't trust her good intentions. It was time for my second bombshell. Those weren't squares that Edward drew. "I know about the diamonds."

A flush rose up on her cheeks and her eyes drew together. She was angry and I was even more scared. "That big fucker! My brother has—had a big mouth. He swore he'd never tell. I always knew he couldn't be trusted.

"Yes, yes, yes, I set you up. Sorry about that. You met me when I was almost done having fun playing urban guerilla. I was just about to leave the Weather Underground. I liked blowing things up, but they were getting so serious and self-absorbed. Then I found out about Paula's dad and his wonderful, illicit diamonds. This was business.

247

"She was more than willing to tell me the combination to Daddy's safe. She'd do anything for me, the little slut. You look a little shocked, Warren. You're not used to a woman talking this way, are you?"

I readjusted my face into neutrality. "Veronique, you will always amaze me. Why did you get me involved, back then?"

"I wanted to blow everybody up, but I didn't want the other Weather-freaks coming after me. Besides, I didn't know exactly how to do it without getting wasted in the process. You were the perfect triggerman. I worked on Frank, Ted, and Terry for months to get them excited about blasting apart that dance in Jersey. Your timing was perfect; I was getting a little worried that you'd show up after the event. But you came in and did the job.

"I admit I was hoping you'd go up in smoke, too. But I didn't mind buying you off with a few rocks. Having you alive helped me out. That way I could always point anyone who came after me toward you, the true Judas. Every few years I'd hire someone to track you down. It wasn't that hard."

It was my turn. "That's how you knew where I was. And you sent your brother to rope me in. But why me?"

I was afraid that she'd already decided to kill me, in spite of her story about keeping me on the run. I had way too much information about her. Talking to her beat taking a bullet.

"You're an inquisitive little twerp, aren't you? But I guess you have a right to know. My brother came to Europe and hauled me out of Germany after I got into a little smuggling trouble.

"I already knew you were in Berkeley, from my last skip trace. You are such a loser as 'the Fugitive.' It was easy to find you. I always knew you'd end up in California. It's the only place that far away from your family, and yet crazy enough to

248

suit your eccentric tastes. When I first got back in the States, I saw your new name in the local papers. Boy, the cops were really pissed at you for a while. Good thing that guy confessed and killed himself."

I was confused. "But that happened half a year ago. Edward said you were only over here a couple of months."

She smiled. "I told him to lie to you. He didn't care. After all, in his eyes I was never a suspect. Anyway, I was hanging out in my bro's silly little coven deciding what to do next. Then somehow Roger Black found out about one of my less savory dealings. You'd think a bunch of Satan worshippers wouldn't mind a little smuggling. Besides, I was never a part of the production arm of that kiddie-porn operation. All I did was distribution. Anyway, he was stupid enough to confront me. I drove over that little annoyance around the time I first found out about Steed's will.

"Now Steed was a pain to get rid of! Then I had to wait around until his estate settled. Lately, I realized that my dear brother was starting to get a little suspicious. It was time for him to join the departed.

"Anyway, I figured you'd be the perfect fall guy for this job. And you are. Thank you, Warren."

I should have studied some other martial art. I wish I'd studied under the guy who taught Keanu Reeves all those cool moves in *Matrix*. I needed to be able to throw myself at her, dodge bullets, and nail her right in the face with one lethal kick.

Unfortunately I studied aikido. It's only good as a defensive technique. And she didn't look like she was going to charge me anytime soon.

She zipped up her suitcase with one hand. "Here, Warren,

help me take this outside to my car. Then we can say good-bye and never see each other again."

Sounded better than getting shot right there, so I took her up on it. I walked over to the case. She stepped back two steps. I picked her case up, turned, and headed for the door. If she was going to plug me, there was nothing I could do. Actually, dying might be a relief.

I made it out the door and down the sidewalk to her car. When I turned around she was right behind me, no gun in sight, her hand in the pocket of her raw silk jacket. I could hear her breathing. It was a little labored. She said, "Oh, I forgot my journal. That's not a very good idea. Stay right here. I want to give you a going-away present. I'll be right back."

She turned around and walked back down the walkway toward her little cottage. What kind of trick was this? Then, I got it. She wanted me to run. The cops would keep chasing after me. Or I could be real stupid and go directly to the cops. Then they could ignore my story and throw me in jail. Either way she walks free. I watched her stumble a little as she crossed the threshold of her house. No, I wasn't going anywhere. I'd do the one thing she wouldn't expect. I'd wait for her.

I stood there, waiting. And waiting. And waiting.

CHAPTER FORTY-FIVE

I walked slowly back down the path toward her house. The door was open. I didn't want to startle her, not with my gun in her pocket. I called out her name. Nothing.

I entered and saw no sign of her. There was an odd thumping noise ahead of me. I walked toward it, around her couch.

Her head lay in a pool of her own vomit. Her arms and legs were flailing around. Her eyes were focused far to the right, and were fluttering open and closed. Her head was shaking. This girl was messed up.

Anyone else, I would have rushed over to help. With Veronique, I seriously considered just walking away. But, shit, I couldn't live with myself if I did that. So I strolled over to the phone and dialed 911.

"There's a woman having some sort of a fit in the cottage behind seventeen-eleven Virginia. Hurry."

I set the phone down and stood still for a moment, listening to her hit her head on the floor. Rev. Morrison would call this evidence of God's retribution. Hightower's cult would chant, "We prevailed." But I knew better. There is no God, and no Satan, only the leering Hyena of blind coincidence. I could hear his snarl as he loped through my life once again.

I didn't have much time. I opened her purse. She had already ditched the Hightower ID cards. There was a lovely California License for Veronique Demour with her beautiful face on it, a US passport in that name, airplane tickets to the Cayman Islands, and three credit cards. "Veronique Devour" would have been a more appropriate choice for her new name. I left the license, but took the credit cards and the ticket. I picked up my Beretta and then I walked away.

I knew where they were going to take her: Berkeley General Emergency. I wanted a little more protection before I went sashaying into that pit. Too many cops wandering around. So I went back to my motel room. First, I made a call to an old client, and a former service provider.

He answered, "What?"

"Hi, this is the guy on the Ave with the funny-looking cards. We did business a few years back. I need docs in a particular name, immediately."

"I can have Oklahoma, no picture, in an hour. Double the usual fee. How's that?"

"Excellent. The name is Strephon Demour, eyes dark brown, hair black, five-foot-five." I spelled the name again for him.

"One hour."

I loved people who excelled in their chosen profession. I'd have an authentic-looking out-of-state driver's license very soon. Then I checked with information and got the number for the Oklahoma Department of Wildlife Conservation. They had a nice long prerecorded message. I listened a few times to pick up the accent. I knew to always under-do an accent, "liiike you try'n to geet rid of hit."

It was time for a little makeup and wig adornment. Then I made a quick trip over to Target for a couple of boring beige polyester sports shirts and a light green golf shirt. I got two pairs of dark brown slacks to match. Leather loafers and a thick leather belt finished things off just fine. I also needed some clean socks and underwear. I had to rough the clothes up a little to get that slightly mussed look. Then I was hot to trot. Life goes so much more easily when you're manic.

My man with the ID was ready for me, with a nicely weathered license for only four hundred dollars. I knew it wouldn't stand up under a police record search. What do you want for one-hour service? Strephon Demour was ready to go take care of his sister.

The newly built emergency ward was as chaotic and crowded as its predecessor. I strode up to the front desk, looking very worried. "Howdy, my name is Strephon Demour. You've got my sister, Veronique, in here. She must have come in during the last couple of hours."

The black woman looked up at me, and then down at the files in front of her. "Just a minute, let me check." She found what she was looking for and looked back up. "May I see some form of identification?" I opened my wallet and flashed her my new name.

"Do you have any form of photo identification?"

Don't say too much! "No. Look, I'm here to see if she's all right. How is she? Here, I have one of her credit cards. I bet ya'll will need this, since she doesn't have a speck of insurance."

That got her attention, and there were no more questions about my identity. She took the card and ran it through her machine. When it turned out a winner she looked at me with new affection. "Mr. um . . . Demour. We are very glad to see you. We need you to fill out some forms for us."

Fifteen signatures later, they were ready to let me sit in the waiting room and wait to speak to her doctor. Finally she came out, with thin strawberry-blond hair, deep creases on her forehead, and dark circles under her pale blue eyes. "I'm Dr. Radstone. You are Veronique's brother, I understand."

"That's right, ma'am. How is she?"

"Not good, I'm afraid. I have some difficult news for you, Mr. Demour. Your sister has had a major CVA, a stroke. Because of the sudden onset and the severity of her symptoms, we think that it's a large cardiogenic embolism: a plug made up of plaque that dislodged from somewhere in her cardiovascular system and ended up blocking a main artery in her brain. That blockage cut off blood to nerve cells, which immediately started dying. She came in with seizures, paralysis, both to her right limbs and to the muscles on the right side of her face. She has almost no capacity to speak.

"We've chemically broken up the blockage, but there is extensive damage. And I'm afraid that, if she pulls through this, she will be permanently and severely disabled. I'm sorry."

Music to my ears. I tried to look stricken. "When can I talk to her?"

"She is unconscious right now. We are hoping that she will wake up soon. Is there a number where I can reach you?"

I gave her my cell phone number and left the waiting room, looking as close to crestfallen as I could muster. Life was amazing. I kept remembering what Philip Letour had said, "The wheel will also turn for your adversaries."

In the hospital parking lot I changed my message on my voicemail to say, "You've reached Strephon Demour. I'll be back in Tulsa around the first, but go ahead and tell me what's on your mind, okay?"

I didn't go directly home. What was this journal Veronique was so god-darned anxious to get her hands on? I stopped at Safeway and made a couple of domestic purchases.

It was about eleven at night, and all the lights were off in the house in front of Veronique's cottage. Good. As I walked quietly into the backyard I put on some latex gloves. Her front door was locked. I walked around the cottage and easily opened a side window into her living room.

I hoisted myself in and flicked on my miniature Mag-Lite. I unlocked the front door and left it slightly ajar. Then I looked around. The red book was on a table in the living room. I put it in a gallon-sized, freezer Ziploc bag. I left, with my late-night reading tucked into the back of my pants.

CHAPTER FORTY-SIX

I made two stops before my morning visit to my "po' little sister": one to a drugstore, and the other to a junkie I knew on the Ave. The frightening thing was that the junkie didn't seem at all surprised to see me with brown eyes, black hair, and in polyester. Heroin is not a memory-enhancing drug. I put my purchases in my pocket and headed to Berkeley General.

It was a new doctor the next morning, an attractive, dark-skinned woman about my height, named Dr. Ali. She spoke without an Indian accent. "Your sister is awake. She still cannot speak or move her right arm. Also the right side of her face is flaccid. I am telling you this so you will not be surprised. She looks a little grotesque right now. However, good news, she is able to move her head, and she responds correctly to 'yes/no' questions, so it appears her cognitive functions were not severely damaged."

"Thank God. I was so worried she'd end up a vegetable. How much will she get back?"

"It's much too early to say, Mr. Demour. The important thing is to keep her spirits up. The best progress can only happen if she truly believes that a good life is possible. I know she is very frightened right now, so anything you can do to calm her will make a world of difference to her recovery."

"Oh, I can promise you, ma'am, that I will do whatever it takes to help my little sis out."

She smiled, nodded, and looked impressed at my sincerity. She should have called the cops right then and there, but they don't teach mind reading in med school. "You can only stay a few minutes this first time."

"Just so I can see her, that's all I want."

She handed me over to a cute young nurse's aide in a crisp, starched white uniform. She was named Betsy. She brought me into a room with only two beds in it, and, wonder of wonders, the other bed was empty. The Hyena of Chaos works in mysterious ways. I walked over to the bed. Veronique looked up and shook her head.

The nurse, in her kindness, had backed out of the room, leaving brother and sister to commune.

I bent close to her. The right side of her face sagged and a tear ran out of her right eye. I watched her left hand carefully, keeping out of claw range.

I said, "Hello, sis." She was violently shaking her head and making "Duh . . . duh" noises. In a lower tone I said, "Shut the fuck up, Q, or I'll just walk out of here, and you can be a fucking rutabaga for the rest of your many, long years."

She stopped moving and watched me fiercely with her one good eye.

I thought back to what she had done to ruin my life. I

added up the long string of murders she had committed. Then I reached into my pocket and held out a little pocket mirror I'd picked up at Long's Drugs before this visit. I kept it in front of me, so no one looking in could see what I was doing. I angled it so Veronique could see the wasteland that once was her face.

I said, "You're never going to be able to say anything but 'Duh . . . duh' again. Your face will always look like this. Your right arm will wither. Now I've got one and only one deal. You confess, and you get me off the fucking hook for these murders and I might be able to give you what you long for." I reached into my other pocket and showed her the syringe I held in my hand. "There's enough heroin in here to put you to sleep, so that you'll never wake up. No more paralysis, no more 'duh . . . duh.' Just deep sleep forever. You think about my deal. I'll be back later."

I was heading for the door when I heard, "Duh . . . duh!" I looked around. She nodded as hard as she could. Life is good.

I met Dr. Ali out in the hall. I said, "I think I've cheered her up a bit. When can I come and visit again?"

"Thank you, Mr. Demour. I can't tell you how much that's going to help. Come back this afternoon, and maybe you can stay a little longer. We'll see. Visiting hours are three to five, but we will work with your schedule.

"Before you leave, our administrator, Mr. Benson, wanted to have a word with you. Betsy, can you show Mr. Demour to Mr. Benson's office?" It was that fresh young chick again. I watched her backside as we made our way through the corridors.

Finally, she swung around, perky and sweet, and said, "Here we are. Have a fine day, Mr. Demour."

"I'll do my best, Betsy. Thank you."

Mr. Benson needed to go on a diet. When he got up to greet me, he looked like a top. He had a very large waistline, and then everything sloped away from his belt buckle. Thin legs flapped against his gray worsted suit pants. A pointed head stuck out of his open collar. He slowly spun around his desk to shake my hand. His grip was wet and weak. We did the usual superficial chat crap while he settled back into his leather Thomasville recliner. I perched on the unpadded chair in front of his mahogany power altar.

The conversational dance began. "The weather was . . ." "My sister was . . ." "Blah, blah, blah." Finally I got tired of it. "So what did you want with me, Mr. Benson?"

"Yes, well. It is about your sister's care, of course. We so appreciate you coming out of nowhere, as it were, to help. But it's about the credit card you gave us."

"Yep."

"Well, it only has a fifteen-thousand-dollar limit, and we have already far exceeded that."

"Oh, is that all? Look, my sister's care is worth the world to me. I've got a couple more of her cards right here. Why don't I give them to you, right now. You can keep them for her."

He was delighted to fondle the plastic. I was about to make him a lot more happy. "Look, I know this treatment is going to be a long-term affair. I've been with your staff for two days, and I trust you all completely. My sister has eight hundred thousand in one of her accounts. Would it work for me to give you access to that account, and you could just draw out the money as you needed it?"

He beamed. "That is an excellent idea. We can provide a thorough accounting every week of our expenses."

"I'm sure that won't be necessary. I do have one little favor to ask. It would be right nice if she could be by herself in the room she is staying in. She's a very private person."

"No problem at all, Mr. Demour. No problem at all."

"You can leave the other bed in there. I might want to stay for longer periods of time with her as she gets better."

"Fine, very fine. We are more than glad to accommodate your needs. Is there anything else?"

"No, I reckon that's about it."

He actually rubbed his hands together. I couldn't wait to visit the men's room and wash his slimy sweat off me. I got up to leave.

He said, "Do you want to give me that account information now?"

"No, Mr. Benson. I'll need to talk it out with my sis, but I'm sure she won't mind. After all, it's all for her own good, right?"

"Right!" Big smile. What a creep.

CHAPTER FORTY-SEVEN

Next, I needed police protection—that is, protection from the police. So I drove back to my Super 8 Motel command central, cleaned up the pizza boxes, and called the only cop I could trust.

"Yo, dude. Let's rap."

"Where?"

"Skates, head north on foot."

"Twenty minutes"

"That's a big ten-four."

Back to the scene of Veronique's staged murder attempt. A blank gun. That's why I kept dreaming about popguns. Something must have registered in my unconscious about the soft sound of that shot.

I settled down on one of the benches that faced the bay and the Golden Gate. It was a sunny day with a light breeze. I watched a sailboat race, sweeping across the sparkling water, multicolored spinnakers aloft like giant hot-air balloons tethered to a hull.

Mac walked right past me. This disguise worked!

"Dude!"

He turned and look at me, rather annoyed. Then his face changed. He smiled. "Good job, Warren! No wonder we couldn't find you. You look normal."

"The day that a golf shirt is normal to me is the day I cash it in. I have never owned one of these before."

Mac said, "I've got an extra set of clubs at home, if you want to go out and play a few holes."

"Kill me first. Enough clever banter. Mac, you are about to become Berkeley's top crime fighter."

"I get to arrest you? Cool. 'You have the right to remain silent . . .' "

"Remain silent yourself, asshole, and read this. I don't care if your fingerprints are on it." I opened the Ziploc bag and dumped the red journal in Mac's lap. As he read, he'd make comments that were very satisfying to me, like, "Jesus." and "Shit!" and "Where the hell did you get this?" I wouldn't answer any questions until he finished the very short and violent tale.

Then I said, "So here's the dope, Mac. The killer is laid up with a stroke in Berkeley General. There isn't a lot left of her. She can't speak or move one hand and she looks like one of God's biggest mistakes. But she can communicate by nodding; she is cognizant of what's going on around her, and she wants to confess to all these crimes."

He was pissed. "Hey, jerk, by giving me this book you just royally screwed the chain of custody here. I assume you don't

264

want to be brought in as a witness. So how the hell am I supposed to know about all this?"

"You tell anyone that asks that you have a friend named Betsy who works at Berkeley General—"

Mac interrupted. "Hey, I do know a Betsy that works at Berkeley General. I used to date her. She was really cute, but conceited."

I hate young people. Especially young men who can score with foxy, white-coated nurses' assistants and then dump them. If I could just have one month as a twenty-five-year-old . . . Oh well, back to business.

"Good, Mac. I'm happy for you. Call her up. Get her talking, especially about the poor lady brought in yesterday, and her wonderful brother. Then, chalk it up to men's intuition, you decide to go over to make sure the poor sick lady's dwelling was secure. You find the door ajar. You're afraid that a crime was in progress, so you go in to make sure no one was burglarizing the place. You find this book open on the dining room table. While walking past you see the words 'psychic nut,' and become suspicious. The rest is history."

He nodded. "Very neat, Warren. You should have been a DA. Anyway, once I have a good reason for possessing this book, all I have to do is show it to a judge. It should only take a couple of hours to get a search warrant and an arrest warrant."

I said, "Good. The hard part is going to be getting the confession. Here's how I want you to set it up . . ."

At three I was back to visit my "sister." I was getting the royal treatment now. A new nurse was more than willing to leave me alone with her. I leaned over Veronique's bed and, in a tone low enough so that only she could hear, I said, "Damn, you're ugly. Do you want to see yourself in the mirror again?"

She shook her head no.

"So here's the deal, sis. In a couple of minutes some cops are going to come in. They are going to show you your red journal and ask you to confess. I'm going to be hiding in the other bed, with the curtains drawn around me, but I will be able to see your head nod or shake. Do the right thing, and maybe in an hour this whole nightmare will be over for you. Are you with me?"

She nodded.

I climbed onto the next bed and pulled the curtains so that I couldn't be seen. Veronique's head was still in my sight. I was just in time. I could hear the protests from Dr. Ali from the hallway.

"You do not have a right to barge in here, warrant or no warrant. This is my patient and she is . . ."

The door opened. A gruff voice said, "Dr. Ali, we can haul her ass out of here if we want to, and down to the station. I don't think that would be very healthy for your patient. Just work with us here. All we're going to do is ask her a few questions. Then she can rest or whatever you want her to do. Deal?"

Ali said, "I don't like it one bit. Five minutes, and that's all, gentlemen. Then I want you out of here, understand?"

"Five minutes will be more than enough. Thank you, Doctor." She must have left the room because the next thing I heard was the door shutting and that same low voice saying, "Bitch."

I heard Mac say, "Let it ride, Jerry. Let's get this thing done with. Do you have the questions?"

266

Jerry said, "Yeah, let's go. Turn the camera on." Then in a more official voice, "This is an interview conducted in room three-twelve of Berkeley General Hospital in Berkeley, California. Present are myself, Lieutenant Gerald Fisher, badge number 7734 doing the interviewing, and Officer James McNally, badge number 1133, videographer. We are both officers in the Berkeley Police Department. Also present is Ms. Veronique Hightower aka Veronique Demour, a Caucasian female. This interview is pursuant to an investigation of case number H-11887. Today's date is Sunday, September seventeenth, 2004 and the time is fifteen-fourteen. Confirming the time stamping on the tape."

Mac said, "Confirmed."

Jerry said, "Hello, Ms. Hightower. We have some questions to ask you. The man with the video camera is Officer James McNally. Do you understand that this session is being videotaped?"

She nodded.

He read her Miranda rights and asked if she understood.

She nodded.

"Now look, I just want to make sure you understand your situation. You are a suspect in a felony murder investigation. We have a warrant for your arrest. You could get the death penalty for this crime. I repeat, I can bring a lawyer in here at no charge to represent you. Do you want me to do that?"

She shook her head no.

He said, "No one can say this gal was deprived of her rights. Ms. Hightower, do you swear that the information you are about to give me is the whole and complete truth and contains no lies or false information?"

Again the nod.

"Okay, now I will need to ask you some questions to

267

confirm that you are of sound mind to do this interview. Am I holding up three fingers?"

She shook her head no.

"Am I holding up five fingers?"

She shook her head again.

"Am I holding up four fingers?"

She nodded.

"Is Bill Clinton the president of the United States?"

She shook her head no.

"Is it springtime?"

She shook her head no again, and half of her face looked annoyed.

"Are you in San Francisco?"

She shook her head harder.

"Look, ma'am, I know this is annoying. Just a couple more and then I assure you the questions will get more interesting. Is this a pen?"

She nodded.

"That's enough of this crap. Here, did you write in this journal?"

She nodded.

"Is all the handwriting in this journal yours and only yours?"

She nodded.

"It says here that you drove a stolen car over a man and killed him. Did you do that?"

She nodded.

"Was his name Richard Steed?"

She shook her head no.

"Oh, wait a minute. That was the other one. Was his name Roger Black?"

She nodded.

"And then you pushed Richard Steed off the cliff?"

She nodded.

"We found some nuts in a plastic bag in your purse. Is it true that you bought them in Mexico from a man named Anthony Mulhaven?" Nod. "You knew they were highly poisonous?" Nod. "You used them to poison Ella Fletcher?" Nod. "And then you burned down her cabin." Nod.

I heard a long sigh. Then Jerry said, "You're a real piece of work, aren't you?"

She nodded.

"And you shot your brother."

Nod.

"And Warren Ritter helped you out."

She vigorously shook her head no.

"Sure, he lent you his gun, but he had no idea what you were going to do with it."

Again a strong "No!" shake.

"Okay, okay. You shot your brother with a gun you stole from Warren Ritter's storage locker."

Nod.

"And you tossed some Barbados nutshells on the floor to set him up, and then called to tip us off, right?"

Nod.

Dr. Ali began knocking on the door.

"Last question. Did you do all these murders alone, or did someone help you in any way?"

She didn't move her head.

"Oh, shit. That's not the right way to ask it. Did you work alone and without any help?"

She nodded as I heard the door open.

Ali said, "Enough, gentlemen. She is completely exhausted. Now leave right now, do you understand?"

Jerry again, "It is fifteen twenty-seven and this interview is concluded."

I saw the doctor move around Veronique, muttering and asking if she was all right. Q nodded once again. Finally everyone left.

Veronique patiently waited for me to kill her.

CHAPTER FORTY-EIGHT

fter everyone left I swung my legs off the bed and walked over to her. "We're almost done here, Q. The only thing I need is the password to your Cayman Island account. I'm sure you understand my motive here, pure greed. It's what motivated so much of your actions."

She nodded. I was beginning to get a taste of her psyche: a bitter metallic taste. She had no heart at all.

"Is the password all numbers?"

No motion.

"Letters and numbers?"

No motion. What else could it be?

"Words?"

A very slight nod.

"Words and numbers?"

A strong nod.

I started running down the alphabet and got nods for C, A, P, E, C, O. Then I saw it.

"Cape Cod 1969?"

She nodded and made that half smile.

The cabin by the beach, the rain, the Mexican coffee, and a delicious weekend of lovemaking. And it was important enough to her that she used it to protect her fortune. What a complicated creature she was. Just when I decide that she's a monster, this sweet, sentimental side comes out. Truly unknowable.

I took my cell phone out and dialed the number I'd written on a card. I punched in the account number, and then had to keep looking at the phone pad to punch in the password: 2273 263 1969. It worked, I was in. I hung up.

"By my count you have murdered at least eight human beings, Veronique, not to mention completely screwing up my life. So I have some good news and some bad news. It's the same news. I'm not going to kill you.

"You should have listened better. I said I *might* be able to help you, and I said confess and *maybe* your nightmares would be over in an hour. I never said that I would help you. I can help you, but I won't. I was dead wrong about your nightmares. They're just beginning."

I turned around and walked out, her guttural "Duh . . . duh . . . duh" echoing behind me. That, I could translate.

I was having an audience with the king of sleaze. "So, Mr. Benson, here's the situation. I've got to leave town, and I'm going to have to leave the care of my little sister in your capable hands. I want her on permanent suicide precautions. She still has one good arm, and I'd hate to see her die in one of her darker moments because of a lack of protection by your hospital staff."

The snake nodded. "I assure you, sir, we will make sure that does not happen!"

"Good. Now, you have a great responsibility in this matter. I need you to hire the best criminal attorney you can find to represent my innocent sister against these ridiculous trumped-up charges. They have the wrong person. They're accusing her of being some Hightower woman. Ask for every extension and delay as long as possible. The lawyer you hire must do everything in his power to keep her here, where she will be safe and well cared for

"Now, I know this is out of the scope of your usual practice. You will need to be reimbursed for these extraordinary expenses. As long as you keep her here, healthy, and out of jail, you may give yourself whatever annual five-figure bonus you feel you deserve, no questions asked, and I will feel no need to notify the IRS about our little arrangement. Spare no expense on her care and on her defense."

He beamed and said, "I assure you that you will be more than satisfied with my services."

"I have a little favor to ask. She let me know she'd like a mirror mounted above her bed, so she can monitor her progress."

"Oh, that's no problem at all!"

Then I stood up and walked up to the edge of the desk. I towered over him. He looked up, alarmed. I said, "I've got one more thing to tell you. If she dies, or kills herself, or gets hauled off to prison, your sleigh ride ends. And if I get one hint that you tried to embezzle the whole nest egg, you will not live out the year. Are *those* terms clear to you?"

He gulped and nodded.

CHAPTER FORTY-NINE

I drove back to the motel and took a long shower. I washed off the sleaze, the evil, and the playacting. Then I started to cry, remembering the Veronique I'd loved. A figment of my imagination, but such a precious figment. I thought about her password. Somehow I must have meant something to her.

I thought about the Furies, and how they wept when they heard Orpheus sing his plea to be reunited with Eurydice. I was a weeping Fury. I had done my job. A just punishment for all those murders had been meted out. But it was a terrible job, and I felt like shit.

I spent a long time in that shower trying to live with what I had done. My entire disguise washed down the drain. I'd returned to my normal looks, the familiar disguise that I took myself to be. I was a free man again, or as free as I ever was.

The stooped guy behind the counter looked at me carefully as I paid my bill. I imagined he was trying to place me. He might be worried that his memory was playing tricks on him again.

I took my bike back to Al's, locked up my Dave Ellbruck ID cards and put the Warren Ritter ID back in my wallet. Then I walked home.

That walk gave me time to think. Who was I now? I'd romanticized my life during all the years on the run. I'd stoically borne guilt for murder: the greatest sin there is. I'd struggled to justify my crime by thinking about the lives I had saved. And not just in Fort Dix.

After that explosion, the Weather Underground never again took a human life. I felt my act was somehow directly responsible for that, and I could take a strange pride in that fact. Someone had once said, "A fact is not a truth until you love it." I had loved that fact of my crime into a heroic truth.

Now it turns out I was just a pawn in some crazy sociopath's scheme to grab some jewels. I was a clueless henchman in a diamond heist, that's all. It made thirty years of flight seem pretty meaningless. I had to retire the image of the brave but lonely revolutionary, riding alone across the land, with his noble cross balanced on the back of his bike.

So what *was* the purpose of it all? Chaos and meaninglessness? Life's a bitch and then you die? Everything looked bleak.

But I've got to tell you I liked bleak a whole lot better than Rev. Morrison's God who "knows when you've been bad or good, so you better be good for goodness sake." I would never be good enough for that God. Though a small part of me longed for Morrison's surety. Ah, to be so unquestionably devoted. 'Tis a consummation devoutly to be wished.

276

And I preferred this feeling of lost pointlessness over the worship of Edward's Crown Princes of Hell, who prompted me to prevail at all costs, grab all the gusto, and take no prisoners. I admired the Fellowship of the Arising Night's passion, but at the end it felt like self-will run riot.

I didn't want either the dominion of the Almighty or the dominion of the Ego. I just wanted to know why all this bad stuff was happening to me.

God, Warren, just shut up! Stop trying to figure out the meaning of life. All this chewing was just a vain attempt to avoid facing facts. Fact one: I just condemned a woman who I once loved to a fate worse than death. Fact two: I felt rotten about it. Fact three: I lived a lie for thirty years. Then there was fact four: I missed that girl with the dog.

"Hello, Warren."

"Hello, Sally. I miss you. So how about dinner together, sometime?"

"You're a pain in the ass, Warren."

"Yep, but I'd sure rather be a pain than a memory. Sally, I want to see you."

She lashed back, "Sure you want to see me. And I want to see you. But what happens when you lie again, or when you finally decide it's time for that bike ride up to Alaska? I already told you, I can't afford that kind of betrayal."

Something snapped, and I stopped trying to manage the situation. "You're right. You can't afford to be hurt again. You can't afford to be let down or deceived. So go pet your damn dog, sip cappuccinos with Heather and sleep atone at night. Because you might be absolutely correct. I might leave you, and I might lie to you, and for sure sooner or later one of us is going to die. It's stupid to love me because abandonment is guaranteed.

"By all means, play it safe! The only damn reason to stay with me is fear. Fear that, when you are taking your last breaths, you'll be eaten up with regret because you chose safety over love."

There was a long pause. Then a chuckle. "You're a smooth-talking pain in the ass." Then another silence. "But, I guess you're *my* smooth-talking pain in the ass. What are you doing tonight?"

"Driving over to your place."

"Good."

I thought the conversation was over. But then she said, "And Warren, Heather called. She won't be back until late Monday night. I guess it's time. Why don't you bring your toothbrush with you?"

A Historical Note

History in Warren Ritter's universe is very similar to our own. However, a few tiny details differ, and need to be noted. Anyone searching for the Fellowship of the Arising Night, Berkeley General Hospital, the Tarot of the Dark Sun, Ed's Chevron Truck Stop Café, or the hidden coal room at the Euclid Apartments is bound to get frustrated.

My portrayal of the satanic sect is completely a product of my own odd imagination. It in no way represents an accurate portrayal of the Church of Satan or any other sect or group who worships the dark side. However, it's a lot more accurate than information from some fundamentalist Christian groups who lie about satanic cults participating in rape, torture, and violence. None of those alleged abusive acts have ever been proven to be based in fact.

Veronique, the Traveler, Frank Walters, and Paula are all inventions. In reality, the Greenwich Village brownstone that the Weather Underground inadvertently blew up belonged to Catherine Wilkerson's parents. Her father owned a radio station, and never imported diamonds. Catherine and Kathy Boudin lived through the explosion. Terry Robbins, Ted Gold, and Diana Oughton died in the explosion. I don't think Bernadette Dohrn was even in town. Otherwise, the history about the Weather Underground and the sixties is fairly accurate. I am solely responsible for the content, and I apologize for any inaccuracies.

A picture of an anonymous Weatherwoman does appear in Jeremy's Vernon's excellent book about the Weatherman, *Bringing the War Home*. Apologies also to whoever was in that photograph for making you into Veronique.

Finally, I want to urge the reader to ignore any medical strategy that Warren Ritter uses to deal with his manic-depression. He is an eccentric and unstable man. These medications are very dangerous and not something to play around with. To treat any mental illness, please consult an experienced physician and only take medication under your physician's exact direction.